PROBLEMS

About fifteen minutes later Henry sidled up and said, "I hear your brother knocked up my sister."

I hate that expression: knocked up. I mean, I know it's just a colloquial expression and shouldn't be taken literally, but it still bugs me. I just glared at him. Then I said, "Henry, listen, will you swear absolutely not to tell anyone—even your parents?"

"Even my parents! Why should I tell *them*?"

I guess nobody talks to their parents much. "No reason," I said. "Just . . . well, you know, if you're not really careful, these things leak out and it would be better—"

NORMA KLEIN grew up in New York City where she still lives with her biochemist husband and two young daughters. In 1960 she graduated from Barnard College with a degree in Russian, followed by an M.A. from Columbia in Slavic Languages. She is the author of many published short stories, an adult novel, GIVE ME ONE GOOD REASON, and MOM, THE WOLFMAN AND ME, and SUNSHINE.

It's Not What You Expect

Norma Klein

AVON
PUBLISHERS OF BARD, CAMELOT AND DISCUS BOOKS

AVON BOOKS
A division of
The Hearst Corporation
959 Eighth Avenue
New York, New York 10019

First Avon Printing, May, 1974
Seventh Printing

AVON TRADEMARK REG. U.S. PAT. OFF. AND
FOREIGN COUNTRIES, REGISTERED TRADEMARK—
MARCA REGISTRADA, HECHO EN CHICAGO, U.S.A.

Printed in the U.S.A.

For Jean—
the last two lines of
Charlotte's Web

Contents

It's Not What You Expect

Chapter One ⚓ A Picnic
with Oliver

Oliver and I are going on a picnic today. I'm glad he suggested it. It makes you feel there's at least something you can get out of this beautiful weather. We could go down to the swimming pool, but I don't like it too much. The trouble is it's sort of a country club type of thing with boys pushing girls into the water and these really dumb girls spending all day oiling each other up with suntan lotion and pretending to read some book that you know they'll never finish. I hate all that. I only go if I'm really desperate on really boiling hot days.

Oliver and Mom were in the kitchen fixing the picnic lunch. Oliver was making smoked oyster sandwiches on *kommisbröt* with Boston lettuce.

"No mustard for me, folks," I said, sitting down.

I have to explain that when you go on a picnic with Oliver it's not one of your peanut butter and jelly and lemonade in a thermos type of affairs. It's more like cold roast chicken and purple grapes and sandwiches you never heard of because Oliver invented them. Or he read about them in *Gourmet Magazine*. Oliver is a great reader of *Gourmet Magazine*. If some little old lady writes in with this crazy recipe to commemorate her long lost cousin, Mehitabel, who disappeared in World War One—that's the kind of recipe Oliver will decide to make. And actually will make.

Oliver is my twin brother. He's fourteen, like me, but he looks about thirty years old. He always has, even in baby pictures. He has this very round sort of cherubic face with a big mop of curly reddish hair and these big round tortoise shell glasses. Somehow he looks like a bachelor. I don't know exactly what I mean by that, but you just know by looking at Oliver that he will always be a bachelor. He'll grow up and have this very neat apartment with a huge baby grand piano and all sorts of books and a great kitchen since he's such a good cook. Maybe he'll invite me over for dinner sometimes. I hope so. I have the feeling at times that Oliver and I may be coming to the parting of the ways. Maybe it's always that way with twins. We were close as babies, and I'd say that even now when we have separate rooms we're still close, but I guess that has to end.

"Mom, are you using all those eggs?" Oliver said. "I'd like to devil a few."

"Oh, devil a few, Ol," Mom said. "Live high."

Mom looked more cheerful this morning. "Carla, will you get Ralph out of bed? I mean—what is this? Breakfast at noon?"

Ralph is my older brother. He's eighteen. "He was probably out late," I said. "It's his vacation, anyhow."

"He's supposed to mow the lawn."

"Oh come on—he never will," I said.

Oliver said, "We'll ask Lester Stollingwell,

Mom. We're going down past there for the picnic."

"I thought they went away already."

"Well, we'll see."

It was a perfect June day. I was glad we were going past the Stollingwells'. It's kind of deserted there and quiet at almost any time of year. The Stollingwells have this great deal, actually. During the winter they run a ski lodge. You have to drive a bit for the skiing, but it's such a nice place that I guess people just come there. Then for the other six months of the year when there's no skiing they go someplace else and just have a vacation. I wouldn't mind living like that.

They were still there, having lunch when Oliver and I came by. Oliver mentioned about the lawn.

"Sure, I'll give it a roll," Lester said. He's about Ralph's age, but sort of dumb-seeming. I don't especially like him.

Mrs. Stollingwell is this very nice person. She's kind of dumpy with a very tan, seamy-looking face. I used to think she was old enough to be her husband's mother, but now I think she just has that kind of face, probably from being out in the sun so much. "Kids, want some pie?" she asked us. She's the type who makes her own bread and pie, which are delicious.

"No, we're going on a picnic," said Oliver. "Is that okay?"

Technically, you have to get the Stollingwells' permission when you use their land for a picnic, I

13

guess because they don't want it overrun with strangers. But they always say yes.

"Are you leaving soon?" I asked.

"In a week," Mrs. Stollingwell said. "*If* we ever get packed. Lord, what a lot of stuff!"

"Have a good trip," I said.

Oliver and I walked down by the brook and found a nice cool place under a tree. We ate like pigs and then Oliver took out his flute and started to play. He's lucky that he plays an instrument you can just bring along on a picnic like that. I mean, I couldn't very well lug my cello on a picnic. While he was playing, I climbed up the tree. I like Oliver's playing. He plays in this very calm, sweet way, very peacefully. I climbed as high as I could and found a comfortable niche and just listened.

It's funny. I sometimes used to wish I had a sister, but now I'm glad I have brothers. There are these girls at school, like even my best friend, Marsha Peterman, an only child, who thinks of boys as another race practically. Whereas I guess having shared a room with Oliver till we were ten and having taken baths with him and all that, I realize boys aren't any different. It probably takes some of the mystery away, but I don't think I'm the type who likes mystery that much on the whole.

"Carla?"

"Umm?"

"Listen, I just had an idea."

"Ya?"

14

"Come on down, will you? I can't talk to you if you're in a tree."

"Why not? I can hear you perfectly well."

"I can't even see you! Where are you?"

I bent back a branch. "Hi! What's the idea? Speak up."

"Let's start a restaurant."

"Where? What do you mean?"

"I have it all planned out," Oliver said. Let me say that in fact when Oliver gets ideas, they always seem to come all planned out. It's discouraging. "We'll use the Stollingwells' house," he said.

"But, like, who will run it and do the cooking and stuff?" I said.

"Us. I'll cook and you can be *maitre d'hotel* and, well, maybe Ralph can help in—"

"Ya, but you need more than three people—you need waiters and lots of things."

"So? There're plenty of kids around here who would be glad to earn some money. That won't be any problem."

"But how about school? Are we going to drop out?"

"No, it's just for the summer, dope. The Stollingwells come back in the fall. We'll just do it for July and August and maybe part of September, if it goes well. It'll be great, Car. I've been thinking about the menu. We'll offer a few cold soups. We can make them at the beginning of the week. Then maybe five *entrées*, all made fresh to order. Very simple, but with extremely good ingredients. No *á la carte*, that's too much bother. We can charge . . . oh, maybe eight dollars a dinner."

"What? Eight dollars! You're kidding! Who'd pay eight dollars a dinner?"

"Plenty of people. Look, we're too far from Boston and there's no place to eat around here—and there's plenty of people with money, or guys who want to take girls out on dates."

"For eight dollars a head?"

"Sure! That's not much. They can bring their own wine so they'll save right there. Eight dollars for a really superb French meal is nothing. It's a bargain. Think of all the people driving past here on their way to concerts and stuff. They'd love a nice, friendly, cosy place to stop off and eat. We'll have black napkins—"

"Oliver, will you wait one second? First of all, how do you know the Stollingwells will let us? What'll they get out of it?"

"Rent, for one thing. And Mrs. Stollingwell always says she hates to put their cat in the vet's. So we'll take care of her cat free of charge, keep the place in good shape so no one will break in ... I mean, naturally we'll have to ask her. But what do you think? Personally, I think we could make a couple of thousand dollars at least."

I sighed. "I don't know. I just can't believe it. Like, how will people find out about it?"

"We'll put up posters. We'll advertise. Look, you've got to realize we've got the market cornered. There is no place to eat around here except maybe Song Wu's and The Pizza Parlor."

"Maybe that's because no one cares about good food."

"Maybe. Only I think it's because no one bothered to think of this before."

I was silent. I had to admit as an idea it was great. But lots of ideas are great, especially ones that you can't imagine ever happening in real life like this one.

"The hours will be six to nine," Oliver went on. You have to give him credit for thinking this out! All while playing the flute yet! "That way, we'll have time to clean up and not get to bed so late the next day will be killed."

I began climbing down from the tree. "Ol—"

"So, what do you think?" He looked really pleased and excited.

"I think it's a great idea," I said. "*Too* great . . . it's just too great. It won't work."

"Oh come on! Since when are you such a pessimist?"

"I'm not a pessimist, it's just . . . there are probably nine million tiny things you haven't thought of that would make it impossible."

"So, we'll look into it. Look, do you want to spend the summer sitting on your ass all day?"

"No," I admitted, though frankly it didn't sound that unappealing. "I guess up till now I kept thinking we might go to camp after all."

"We discussed all that. I told you *you* could go if you wanted."

"You know I wouldn't go without you."

"Why not? We're not Siamese twins."

"Oh, it's not that. I just would feel funny—only I kept thinking, you know, like Dad would come back and then we could go."

About two weeks ago Dad had moved into an apartment in New York and all Mom would say was he needed time to be by himself. Then Oliver decided we shouldn't go to camp the way we usually do. He said it wasn't right to leave Mom alone, and think of the money. It's nice that Oliver is like that. I must say I've often liked that trait in him. He really is an altruistic person, which I'm afraid I'm not to that extent. Of course, I could have gone and let Oliver stay home with Mom, but that would have made me seem sort of selfish. Also, I thought he was partly right. What would Mom do just hanging around the house for two months since Ralph, even if he's technically at home, is with his girl friend, Sara Lee, all the time? Now, looking at me with his owlish professor expression, Oliver just said, "Wise up, dope."

"What's 'wise up'? They're not getting divorced, are they?"

"How should I know?"

"Well, what do you think?"

"I think . . . no. The odds are against it."

I sighed. "Ya, I kind of think that too. But then, how do you know?"

"You don't, but you don't spend two months just sitting around thinking about it."

"Yeah, I guess."

I followed Oliver back to the Stollingwells, but somehow now that I had started thinking about Mom and Dad, I couldn't concentrate on the restaurant idea so much. Anyhow, the Stollingwells weren't even there so we decided to come back later on to ask.

Chapter Two ❧ How Is this Mother Different from All Other Mothers?

When we got home, I went into my room to unpack my camp trunk. About that, I figured Oliver was right. If I really wanted to go, I should have said I'd go without him. Since I'd decided not to, I ought to make my peace with it. Mom looked in, saw what I was doing, and said, "How was the picnic?"

"Fun," I said. I decided not to mention Oliver's idea until it seemed like something might really happen.

"I'll be in the studio," Mom said and disappeared.

It's funny with Mom. She just doesn't look like a mother. I mean, the mothers around here, to me, all look a certain way which is hard to explain. They all seem to have sort of straight hair, usually loose, and they wear tweedy slacks and white blouses. They usually play tennis or golf very well. Whereas Mom, like Oliver and me, is completely unathletic. For one thing, she's about five feet tall. I got taller than her when I was eleven and now I practically tower over her. She weighs around one hundred pounds so her figure looks more like a ten-year-old boy. Also, her hair is odd.

It's extremely short. I guess you could say boyish except boys wear their hair so long nowadays. She trims it herself with a nail scissors. It looks it. Her hair used to be blond, but lately it's been getting sort of grey. I wish she'd dye it, actually. All the mothers here do, so if your mother doesn't, it makes her look around eighty. Oliver always says Mom shouldn't dye her hair, that he likes her the way she is, but I think she should.

The other thing with Mom is that she really doesn't do that much. But she's an extremely talented person. Like, for one example: When we used to live in New York and Oliver and I shared a room, Mom once painted our whole room—walls, ceiling, everything—with this great mural of all kinds of wild beasts, not scary but very sweet and funny-looking. We loved it. It was different from anything you ever saw. Of course, when we moved, we couldn't take it along and it seemed a pity that the people who moved in would just cover it over with white paint.

Or like with this dollhouse Dad once made me—Mom has made these fantastic, really beautiful things for it. I mean, like, she gets carried away on things like that and will spend all afternoon making some great couch for the dollhouse. But it never adds up.

Another thing was that at Christmas she used to make these beautiful felt bags and Christmas stockings for all her friends. They would be decorated with patchwork and sequins—much nicer than what you see in the stores. Only she'd never try to sell them or do anything with her skill.

Once she took some of her stuff to a store in New York called The Elder Craftsman that supposedly sells things only by people who are over sixty-five. She said the bags and things were made by her sister, Arlene, who was ailing and couldn't bring them in herself, and they took them and sold a few. (Mom does have a sister, Arlene, by the way, but she's about thirty-five years old, lives on West Eighty-Sixth Street in New York City and is about the most uncreative person you can think of.)

I have this theory about mothers. I mean, you could say what do I know, being only fourteen, but I think kids of fourteen are quite mature today. Anyway, be that as it may, my theory is this: There are two types of mothers. One, the most common type around here, is the type I mentioned before—the tweed slacks, golf-playing type. That type usually has maybe four kids and is a quite good cook (or has a housekeeper who is a good cook), and has a certain sort of house—for instance with a playroom in the basement with a bar, a ping pong table, and indoor-outdoor carpet on the floor. That might sound like a stereotype, but I'm just trying to give you a general idea, and, in fact, you could find lots of families like that around here without even trying.

Then there's Mother Number Two who would be like Marsha Peterman's mother who is a computer programmer and goes to work every day and is kind of perky and odd and doesn't care much about how the house looks and has one or at most two children. Personally, I don't think it matters much which type a mother is, but she

21

should decide *which* she is. Or at least not sit down and *decide* which she is but just *be* one or the other. The trouble with Mom, in my opinion, is that basically she's Type Two, but she isn't really because she never had a job. Yet she isn't really Type One because first of all, she just isn't, and secondly, she is a lousy housekeeper, doesn't believe in servants and isn't, when you come right down to it, such a hot cook. I mean, she can whip up a meat loaf and some chicken or something not too taxing, but when it comes to gourmet things, it's mostly Oliver who does them.

I really don't know if the things about Mom that I've mentioned have anything to do with Dad's going to New York for the summer. It could be some utterly different thing I know nothing about. I mean, you know your parents, but you don't really know them. So these are really just idle speculations which, at least, have kept me busy. I find that I've actually—miracle of miracles—unpacked my whole trunk. I lugged it downstairs into the basement. No, we do not have a bar and a ping pong table, just a lot of old junk, some art materials for Mom, and some carpentry stuff for Dad. It's really quite a wreck down there, if you must know.

"I unpacked," I told Oliver who was in the kitchen making a snack.

"Good work, Hank." Oliver and I always used to kid around when we had a job, pretending we were these two workmen who trim lawns around here, Hank and Sam.

"Hey, Sam, when are we going to speak to the Stollingwells?"

"Tomorrow morning. Only I've decided we should ask Ralph to come if he will."

I made a face.

"I agree, only I have the feeling they'll think fourteen is a bit young."

"Will he do it, though?"

"We'll ask him later."

Oliver had the transistor radio on as he always does when he's in the kitchen. I turned it down a bit. "Ol, you know, I've been thinking—I really think Mom should dye her hair."

He looked at me with his there-she-goes-again look.

"No, I mean, like with this thing with Dad—you know—she might want to go out while he's away and who'll want to go out with her if she looks around a hundred?"

"Go out on *dates?*" He looked like I'd suggested she might want to do a belly dance in the middle of the shopping center.

"Yeah. Not romance-type things—just, like, to the movies and stuff like that. Anyway, I think it would make her feel better—more youthful, you know."

"She looks great the way she is," Oliver said.

"To you, sure. Look, she wouldn't have to dye it some horrible platinum blond—just the color it was before. Marsha Peterman's mother has hers dyed this very natural color, sort of brownish blond that you'd never know wasn't real."

"Then how *do* you know?"

"Well, I saw her doing it, actually. She does it at home."

"But then she'll start all that junk with painting her nails and stinking up with perfume and—"

"Oliver, God, she's going to be forty years old! I mean, like, women of forty wear perfume!"

"Who's going to be forty years old?"

I turned around and there was Mom. I almost died. I wondered if she had heard our whole conversation. "You," I said.

"Right you are." Mom sat down. "Hey, Ol, make us all some great cold soup, will you? I can't face supper tonight."

"Sure. Vichyssoise okay?"

"Great."

Oliver went to the refrigerator and started looking for ingredients. "So, what color are you going to dye your hair, Mom?"

Mom smiled. "You think I should? Really?" You could tell she'd been thinking about it.

He looked at a potato and turned it around in his hand. "Personally, I don't ... but, well, if it could be done so it looked natural ..."

"I was thinking of red, actually," Mom said with this kind of mischievous expression.

"Red!" He looked horrified. "Oh no! God no! Please! Not red, never red. Swear it won't be red."

Mom and I burst out laughing. "Oliver, what's wrong with red?"

"Red dyed hair is so ugly," Oliver said. "Anyhow, for red hair you have to have red eyebrows and all that. Now, don't do it if you're going to look like a wreck."

"I look like a wreck now," Mom said. "What's the difference?"

"No, you don't Mom," I said. I guess I felt guilty for all those things I'd been thinking while I was unpacking the trunk.

She just looked at me and smiled sort of sadly.

Chapter Three ⚡ Sounding Out the Stollingwells

Ralph was great about the Stollingwells. When he wants, he can be quite charming. I suppose it seems sort of phony, but I will admit there are times when it can be of use. In a way Ralph's the only really normal person in our family. At times I've hated him for it, but I admire him too. He's always been good at everything—school *and* sports *and* he has this great girl friend, Sara Lee Takami, that he's been going with since third grade practically. I used to feel bad because he'd treat Oliver and me like a pair of weirdos, just funny kids not worth bothering with. But lately, since his year away at college, he's better, not so snotty. Anyway, Sara Lee is so sweet and shy with this lovely quiet voice and beautiful long straight black hair that I figure there must be something nice about Ralph if she likes him.

When we brought up our plan, at first Ralph ridiculed it to pieces, but Oliver just sat there calmly, as he always does, taking it all and coming back with things. I admire that in Oliver so much. I wish I could be cool. Unfortunately, like Mom, I'm afraid I usually feel so emotionally involved that I know I'll either fly off the handle or burst into tears, which I just hate in myself. Anyhow, after an hour of this drilling, Ralph suddenly said he thought it sounded like a pretty good idea and he'd be glad to "represent" us and "check out the legal loopholes." Ralph intends to be a lawyer, by the way. He loves expressions like "legal loopholes."

So the next morning, even though it was raining, we all drove over to see the Stollingwells. As I say, Ralph was excellent in this totally urbane, suave way. You could tell he was modeling his performance on some lawyer he admires. For one thing, which I thought was rather clever, he addressed himself mostly to Mrs. Stollingwell. I had been thinking that if Mrs. Stollingwell said yes, that would be it. I don't know why it is, but you get the feeling with most married people that there's one person who basically decides everything. It's hard to say why since, from what I've seen, it's not especially the smartest or the loudest person. But in this case I knew it would be Mrs. Stollingwell and it was. At first she was sort of dubious. She's a very slow-talking considered person who you can tell doesn't leap into things at all and for about half an hour I was sure she was going to say no.

"You intend to have people stay over here?" she asked. We were all sitting around the butcher board table in their huge kitchen.

"Oh no," I said. "It's just a restaurant. We just need the kitchen and the dining room."

"The kitchen equipment?" she said.

"Well, we could bring some stuff from home, couldn't we?" I said, looking at Oliver.

"Oh, of course. Our mother has a lot of silverware and tablecloths and things she never uses so that needn't trouble you at all."

"She would let you use them?" Mrs. Stollingwell asked, not meanly, just being curious.

Needless to say, we hadn't mentioned a word of all this to Mom, but Ralph said smoothly, "She's delighted with the plan. The twins thought of it" (Ye Gods, we haven't been called "the twins" in years!) "and Mother was quite amazed at two kids their age being so resourceful. Of course, I would oversee and help in any way I—"

"It certainly sounds resourceful," Mrs. Stollingwell said.

"It sure does," said Mr. Stollingwell.

"Naturally we would pay rent as well as a cut of the proceeds," Ralph said.

"Oh, a cut wouldn't be necessary. My only fear, really, is that, well, you know, this place isn't so grand, really, but to us—"

"Oh, we love your place!" I said. "That's why we thought of it. It's just what we wanted—not fancy, but—"

She smiled and I knew I'd hit the right note. "I fell in love with this place myself when I first saw it. Remember, Frank, that time we first saw this place? It was an old ramshackle thing then. We hadn't added on the extra wing or anything, but I remember I stood there—I was pregnant with Lester at the time—and I just thought: I want to live here."

"Ya, that's right," Frank (or Mr. Stollingwell) said. "Those were her words."

Anyhow, by that point it seemed like the Stollingwells were warming to the plan. They even said they'd try to get back in time to have a meal before it closed. (We'd picked September fifteenth as a good final day since it was a Sunday and just about three months away.) Ralph said we should sign a contract and, even though the Stollingwells demurred at first, I could tell they were pleased at having it all so legal and thorough.

"And is this young lady going to be your chef?" Mr. Stollingwell asked, patting my arm.

I cleared my throat. "Well, actually, Oliver will probably do most of the cooking. I'm going to be *maitre d'hotel.*"

"I see . . . you'll take reservations and all that?" I could see he was somewhat amused at the idea, which bugged me a little. But then he said, "Martha, you know who would love a place like this? The Effings."

"Wouldn't they!" Mrs. Stollingwell beamed. "Yes, I'll definitely call Suzanna. They've always said there is just no place to eat in this whole community. And Myer is *insane* about good food."

Oliver looked at me and grinned. "I hope they love soups," he said. Soups are Oliver's specialty, you see.

"Oh, they're crazy about soup! Myer says he could eat soup all day long! Oh, he'll love it!"

On this note we parted, hoping there would be lots of people like the Effings who would rally round if the restaurant ever got off the ground.

Chapter Four ⚡ Dad's Sex Life
or What Oliver Knew

Sunday, Mom's sister, Arlene, came over for brunch. She had picked up all this great stuff at a delicatessen—pickled herring, fresh bagels, lox, cream cheese chopped up with chives—it was a great feast. I felt starving.

While Mom was out of the room and everyone was kind of looking at whatever parts of the Sunday paper they had grabbed, Aunt Arlene suddenly said, "So, what's this with Daniel?"

Daniel is Dad. I had kind of known we would have to come to that, but since we'd managed to avoid the topic so far, I had hoped we might not. Oliver and I both shrugged our shoulders simultaneously. Sometimes all I have to do is look at Oliver's face to see what I am feeling. This was one of those times. He had a kind of wary, uneasy look.

"He is living at 301 East 78th Street," I said, "if you want to call him up and have lunch with him."

"Why should I call him up and have lunch with him?" asked Aunt Arlene. "What I want to know is why he did it. What is he—going through a change of life or something?"

"We don't know," I said. "We are just the children."

Aunt Arlene gave me a cut-the-crap kind of look. "Who should know better?" she said. "Don't you keep your eyes and ears open?"

"They didn't have any special fights or anything that I can remember," I said. "Did they, Oliver?"

He shook his head.

Aunt Arlene snorted. "Well, all I can say is I hope he's not tangled up with some dumb hippie kid that he met through his counseling job. Those girls are murder these days, let me tell you."

"That's just a stereotype, Aunt Arlene," I said. "Hippies are very nice people a lot of the time."

"Don't give me that! What do you know?"

"Maybe some are a certain way, but it's unfair to generalize. Anyhow, Dad isn't doing anything like that. Is he, Ol?"

Oliver shook his head again. But what kind of shook me up was the look on his face. I guess by now I can fairly well interpret Oliver's range of expressions and the one that sat there briefly was a bit disquieting. Aunt Arlene didn't notice and went back to reading the paper. But I suddenly lost my appetite and set down the half-eaten bagel I had been munching on.

As soon as Oliver and I were alone, I whispered, "What was that expression you had before?"

"What expression?" he said.

"When Aunt Arlene was saying that stuff about Dad and a hippie girl friend. Does he?"

"Let's discuss it later," Oliver said.

There are times when I could kill Oliver. "Tell me!"

"There's nothing much to tell—but anyway, I refuse to talk about it now."

All afternoon I kept having these lurid speculations about Dad and this imaginary hippie girl friend. The reason I worried is this: Dad is a psychological counselor for this college, Monroe. I imagine he's quite a good one. Basically, he's the type that really does identify with kids and their problems and doesn't take a superior know-it-all position. In fact, if anything, his problem, I gather, is almost identifying too much with his students. Once this guy he had been seeing committed suicide and Dad almost had a nervous breakdown. Everyone kept telling him it certainly wasn't his fault. This guy had had a tremendous number of personal problems and Dad had been going crazy trying to get his course load lightened, speaking to his parents, the dean at the school, everybody. I mean, he really should have had a completely clear conscience. But he still felt so sick about it that he could only eat soft boiled eggs for almost a month. When Dad is worried, he gets what they call a nervous stomach and can hardly eat anything.

There was this one girl who I always had the feeling had a crush on Dad. She was sort of a phony type who would call our house with these supposedly urgent problems. I may be being unfair. Perhaps they really were urgent. Possibly if she'd been a boy, I would have taken another attitude. But I know from my class at school that so many of the girls, if they have a man teacher who is even moderately decent-looking, will just salivate all over him and claim they're in love and all that. So if you have a teacher whose whole job is to discuss personal problems, you have what I'd call a perfect setup.

I hope Dad is not that stupid. I don't believe he is, but then, as I've said, who really knows their parents?

I should add that Dad is not at all bad-looking. In fact, he is rather good-looking. If you want to know what he looks like, I will say that people who wish to flatter him say he looks like George C. Scott and Albert Camus. If you bear in mind that he actually looks like neither of these people and that these remarks are made by people who want to flatter him, you may get the picture. He is of medium height with a scowling intense face and a lot of unruly dark hair which is not that grey yet. Of all these compliments, I might add, he always feels best when people say he is like Albert Camus. Camus is Dad's god and he even has a trench coat like the one Camus is always wearing in the photo on the back of all his books.

That night, I decided, I would sleep in Oliver's room.

Oliver has a bunk bed. He sleeps on the bottom. I used to sleep on top till I had a room of my own. But even now if I'm having trouble sleeping, if I'm worrying about something, I just go in and go to sleep on top of Oliver's bunk bed. I always fall right to sleep. Maybe it's retreating to childhood or something. At any rate, it certainly works very well. I got into pajamas and climbed on top. Oliver was reading, but finally he put his book aside and snapped off his reading light.

"So?" I said.

"Well, first of all you're obviously making a big deal out of something which is actually more or less insignificant."

"Okay—what is it?"

"Second, you know how bad you are at keeping secrets."

This, I must admit, is true. I am very bad at keeping secrets.

"But I'm only going to tell you if you absolutely swear to tell no one, not even Mom or Ralph or Marsha Peterman or anyone."

"Marsha Peterman is away in Europe," I said. I find I tend to do that—not really swear directly. Of all the people mentioned, Marsha is the only one I'd be likely to tell whatever Oliver was about to mention since we discuss our families quite a lot.

"Well, really, it's nothing to do with a girl friend," Oliver said. "Sorry to disappoint you, old girl."

"What is it, then?"

"You may not believe this," Oliver said.

"Oliver!"

"No, it's just that this is something Dad once told me quite a while ago, not in connection with going away, but last year or something. Did you know Mom was the first person he ever slept with?"

"Oh come on!"

"I swear."

"But he was twenty-two when he met her."

"I know."

"That's just not possible," I said.

"Is it the kind of thing someone would make up?"

He had a point there. "But how come? It's too incredible!"

"Well, I gather, for one, sex wasn't as prevalent in that era."

"Ya, but that was like the fifties—not the Stone Age!"

"Also, you have to recall, he had a quite strict family—sort of Puritanical."

This is true. Whereas Mom grew up in New York, Dad grew up in this tiny town in the Midwest and his Mother is this plump, white-haired woman, and his father is this sort of tall, thin, stern man who doesn't speak too much.

"Also," Oliver went on, "he did go to all these all-boys schools where at most they had two dances a year with girls. He even said that the headmaster wouldn't let them see any movie with a woman in it for fear they'd get overstimulated."

"You're kidding."

"Seriously. Even if there was one little scene with, like, a Wac or something, not even sexy, it would be cut."

"But how about college?"

Oliver sighed. "Look, I don't really know. I gather he dated people. Only girls didn't then.

You had to kind of snow them, I gather, and maybe he was sort of shy."

"It's still quite incredible," I said.

"Well, it's true."

I was silent for some time, contemplating all this. "Well, then—oh, oh, the light is beginning to dawn—you think because he didn't then, he wants to now?"

"I don't know that for a fact," Oliver said.

"Oh God!" I said. "That is really disgusting!" I sat up, I felt so mad.

"What is? His not doing it before or his wanting to do it now?"

"Both! I mean, you don't just wait twenty years till you're forty almost!"

"Listen, Car, I knew I shouldn't have told you all this. It's just idle speculation. There is no proof at all."

"Oh God! I'm never getting married! This is so depressing—. Hey, I have an idea."

"What?"

"Let's have Aunt Arlene just go over there to his place one day or one night unannounced. Then she can report back to us if a girl was there."

"Carla! You are really incredible. Isn't he entitled to a private life?"

"No!" I practically yelled.

"Well, I'm having no part of any schemes with Aunt Arlene. Count me out.".

"Spoilsport." But, thinking about it, I guessed Oliver was right. It's true, there was no proof and I do have this tendency to get carried away. "Hey, Ol?"

"Yeah."

"Did Ralph speak to Mom yet about the restaurant thing?"

"Not that I know of."

"Well, let's do it tomorrow, morning, okay? We ought to sort of clear it."

"Sure."

"You sound sleepy."

"I am sleepy."

"Night, Ol . . . sweet dreams."

"Same to you."

Trying to go to sleep, I thought about what Oliver had said. Oliver is right. I must stop jumping to conclusions. This is a bad habit. Can you saunter to conclusions? If so, that is what I must do. The hippie girl friend is quite possibly not real at all. I must admit, however, that I was taken aback by the news of Dad's lack of girl friends prior to his meeting Mom. As I have mentioned, Dad is quite good-looking and I would have assumed otherwise. True, as Oliver says, things may have been different then. That different?

It certainly seems to me a great mistake. I would say it was foolhardy, except that I have been told I have an overly great tendency to judge other peoples' actions. For my own part I will say that I would never marry the first person I slept with. Marsha and I have discussed this at length and have decided we will have at least six affairs before getting married. I am not getting married until I am at least twenty-five and will have my first child at thirty. Marsha isn't getting married until she is thirty and will not have her first child until she is thirty-five. I think that might be stretching it a bit, but I admire her sense of restraint. All things come to those who wait, as they say.

However, with Dad it may have been different. Maybe Mom swept him off his feet. Maybe, having waited so long, he was a goner once he tried it. There are many possibilities and it really does no good to speculate. I have decided to reserve judgment until I see Dad's apartment. Possibly in a few weeks Oliver and I will go in and spend the weekend there. Dad has sublet an apartment from a friend and I would be curious to see it. You might say that if there is a hippie girl friend he would hardly be likely to have her in evidence for such an occasion. However, I believe I might be able to scent the atmosphere. I consider myself a good judge of the lay of the land. I will keep my eyes and ears open, as Aunt Arlene said. That will be better than sending others in my stead.

I admire Oliver's ability not to give a damn. I hate to say it, but maybe boys are different. Privately I have sometimes hoped that if Oliver ever loses his cool, I will be around to see it.

It doesn't seem too likely.

Chapter Five ⚡ Mom Is
a Chicken and Says Yes

Monday is Mom's day for being a chicken.

When Oliver and I went into her room after breakfast to tell her about the restaurant, she was getting into her costume. "Can you spare a minute, Mom?" said Oliver.

"Sure," said Mom, pulling on her yellow feathered chicken tights. It did not look like a comfortable costume to wear on a summer day.

Dad was not happy about Mom being a chicken on Mondays. I must say I can see his point. He said—and I quote—it was yet another example of her frittering away her time and energy on outlets that were trivial, not to say nutty.

How it started was this. Last winter, when the big new shopping center opened, there was an ad in the local paper saying they wanted a group of individuals to dress as farm animals to call attention to the fact that the supermarket—a huge one, right in the middle of the center—will be having special daily deliveries of fresh farm eggs, milk, and other products. The idea was that these individuals ("no experience needed" the ad said) would, on nice days, parade around outside the supermarket, making appropriate animal noises and handing out leaflets describing these products. On cold or rainy days they would walk up and down the aisles of the supermarket doing the same thing.

Mom applied for the job, got it (I doubt there was overwhelming competition), and every Monday since then has dressed in her chicken costume and set off. She says she finds it very restful to abandon her identity and be a chicken once a week. She could have been a cow or even a goat, but opted for the chicken. In her costume she looks a little like Big Bird on Sesame Street. Only she is much smaller, of course.

When Oliver outlined our plan about the restaurant, Mom seemed a bit abstracted, as she has for several weeks now. She said yes, that sounded like a great idea, and went to look for the head part of her costume which she doesn't put on till she gets to the center. Mom's abstractedness has some advantages. Partly, I felt she wasn't really thinking of our plan. It was as though we were eight and had asked if we could set up a lemonade stand outside the house. On the other hand, she may not have been listening at all. Possibly if we had said we were setting up a pot joint in the local library, she would have smiled in an identical way and said what a great idea.

"We may have to use a lot of your kitchen equipment," Oliver persisted.

"Great!" Mom grinned. "Now I'll have a good excuse not to cook all summer."

"We'll have to use the freezer too. I don't think the Stollingwells have a separate one." We have a huge freezer in the basement where you can literally put a whole cow cut into pieces and stow it away for the summer.

Mom seemed amenable to everything Oliver said; she usually is.

After she left we sat down to plan details. I had decided our motto should be: Keep it simple. Or, to put it another way: Do not bite off more than you can chew (which seemed an appropriate motto for a restaurant). What I meant was I thought we should stick to very simple good things that Oliver had made millions of times rather than try to snow people with some beaut like veal with fresh pineapple. Oliver is very good at things like veal with fresh pineapple, but I felt the tried and true would be safest. We ended up deciding on three choices of appetizer: melon with prosciutto, *coquilles St. Jacques,* and *quiche Lorraine;* three choices of soup: mushroom broth, *vichyssoise,* and watercress soup; and three choices of entrees: sautéed trout *amandine,* steak with *sauce Béarnaise,* and chicken in lemon sauce. For dessert we decided to be extremely simple and just serve fresh fruit, maybe with some liqueur poured over it.

It is a good thing to remember that when you serve people fresh fruit with liqueur poured over it, they think they are eating something very good and yet it's not much trouble to make. Oliver said he might make some *madeleines* if he could get hold of some *madeleine* pans. These are like butter cookies, only better. They are supposed to carry you back to your childhood. About the fruit, I must admit I had at the back of my mind the fields behind the Stollingwells', where there are some fantastic blackberry bushes that usually ripen just about July and August. There are quite a few raspberries there too. Oliver and I used to go picking and would practically eat ourselves sick. Eating all the blackberries you want is one of the sublime ways to get sick. I recommend it highly.

"*Gourmet* had an article on blackberries last year," Oliver said, looking dreamy.

"No, no—absolutely no," I said. I knew Oliver was contemplating things like Blackberry Fool and Blackberry Crumble which would probably be delicious but the very devil to make. "Just fresh blackberries with sugar and heavy cream," I said. "Or with kirsch or something."

"You're probably right," Oliver said with some reluctance.

I think Oliver and I make a good team. Oliver has great ideas, but he is not always so practical about carrying them out. I believe this is because essentially he is a perfectionist. I have that streak myself, but I also have a practical streak which rules out things like Blackberry Fool. This is very helpful in business endeavors.

We considered our staff. Oliver, of course, would be chef. I would be *maitre d'hotel* which means I would wear a long dress, stand at the front of the restaurant, take reservations, and guide people to their tables. (I am glad I will not have to be a waitress. I was a waitress one summer for a month and it was not an experience I would like to repeat. People are quite rude in the

43

context of ordering food. They change their orders quite a bit or complain if things are not just so.) The question was: who should be waiters or waitresses, as the case may be? After quite a bit of phone calling, we hit on the following combination: Letty and Joyce Pfeifer as waitresses, Henry and Zachary Takami as waiters.

Letty and Joyce are in our school, Letty in our class, Joyce a year ahead. They used to live near us, but they moved to another district. Their mother is in a mental hospital. Their father is friendly with Mom and Dad. Henry and Zachary are the brothers of Sara Lee. They are fifteen and thirteen. Sara Lee said she would help Oliver in the kitchen, chopping things. Sara Lee is immensely neat and I thought that was a good idea.

By Tuesday afternoon Ralph had a contract drawn up with the help of a lawyer who is the father of one of his college roommates. I had to sign it; so did Oliver, Ralph, Mom, and both of the Stollingwells. It was quite an imposing document. Essentially it said we would be responsible if anything awful happened like the whole place burning down. I must say that after signing the contract, I felt rather nervous. What if the whole place *did* burn down? The Stollingwells, however, seemed very pleased at having it all so official. I can't say I blame them.

Ralph said the important thing was not to overextend ourselves. This, I believe, is another way of saying we should not bite off more than we can chew. He said he thought thirty-five was the absolute most we should try to seat since otherwise it

44

would get too noisy and no one would have a good time. He said the most important element in making a good restaurant, apart from the food, is a quiet, restful atmosphere. Therefore there should be only candlelight. He said that for the first week we should expect at most half of capacity and that perhaps not till the third week would we get full capacity. I had the horrible feeling we would get no capacity. I could just see all of us with everything all set up and one lone person eating in the corner. It would be quiet, all right.

We decided to have every Tuesday and Wednesday off. We were going to have Sunday off, but I pointed out that on Sunday lots of people are returning home from concerts so it's almost as big a night as Friday and Saturday. Whereas Tuesday and Wednesday are kind of nothing days so they wouldn't matter so much. Wednesday we would cook a lot of stuff ahead of time like soups and *hors d'oeuvres* and freeze them. Everything else would be cooked to order. Ralph said he would take care of ordering the food. I must say he is being much more of a help than I would have expected. There is, after all, some advantage to having an older brother.

There was the question of the name. Oddly enough, it took about as long to decide on a name as it did to decide on all the rest together. Oliver wanted a French name, of course. Having a French name cuts two ways. On the other hand, as you may have noticed if you know any French, almost anything sounds beautiful in French. I sometimes wonder if French writers can be any good because if they just say, "Hey, look, it's raining out," it sounds so great. After closeting himself with a French dictionary all evening, Oliver came up with: *L'Alouette* (The Lark), *Au Flanc de Coteau* (On the Hillside), *Le Singe Bleu* (The Blue Monkey), and *Au Claire de la Lune* (In the Moonlight). I myself, being of simple tastes, was in favor of Simple Simon's Retreat. At school everyone used to call me Simple Simon because of our last name, and I became rather attached to that nickname. (Almost anything is better than "Car" unless you have a tendency to identify with motor vehicles.) However, Ralph said that sounded too prosaic, too much like Red Apple Rest. At eight dollars a head, he said, people want glamour. I have never paid eight dollars for a meal, but that sounded reasonable. What we finally hit on was *A Coté de Chez Simon* after Proust. Ralph had been reading Proust for his first year French Lit course and Oliver knows how to make great *madeleines*. At that point I was ready to settle for anything.

That night, mulling things over in bed, I had what I think is a brilliant suggestion. We would have a chamber music night once a week. At ten o'clock when people were just finishing or having dessert, Oliver, I, and maybe Letty who plays the viola could play trios. We could sit toward the back so it wouldn't be too loud. Also, we would announce it on our posters so anyone who really hated chamber music would come on another night.

Another minor suggestion I had was to hang some of Mom's paintings in the restaurant. The Stollingwells, nice though they are, have no taste in art. Their taste runs to paintings of mountains in the sunlight, but the kind that show every crag and cranny. Like photos but not as good. Mom's paintings are a little odd, with funny animals and things, a little like Chagall, but I thought they would be nice. The Stollingwells wouldn't mind, I didn't think. Anyhow, I was glad I'd thought of it because Mom was delighted. She looked more cheerful than she had all summer and said she would try and decide which of her creations she liked best.

Chapter Six ⚉ The Grand Opening

The Grand Opening was on July fourth, Friday. Actually, that first night was quite a success, primarily because the parents of all the staff showed up—Mom, Melrose Pfeifer, the Takamis—and they all brought a few friends. So even if we were filled just to half capacity, there was a festive air. We had decided to let people bring their own wine. Melrose Pfeifer brought champagne and kept toasting us. He is not bad.

I did not have so very much to do that first night, but I must say I enjoyed just standing there and overseeing everything. Henry gave a whistle when he saw me in my long skirt and black jersey turtleneck top. I had deliberately worn a turtleneck instead of a scoop neck, but my figure is the type that shows anyway.

I realize I have never mentioned my figure so far. This is probably because I am a bit embarrassed by it. Suddenly at around twelve and a half I started to get a bust and by now I wear a 34 C cup. I hope the end is near. The ironical part is that most girls my age are always stuffing their bras or wishing to be bigger in that area. My problem is the opposite. I always try to stand stoop-shouldered, which is my natural way of standing anyway, and to wear the baggiest possible things. I wear a size twelve blouse, though I am a seven in a dress. However, despite this, the truth will out, as they say. The reason I have a problem is this. Think of a fourteen-year-old girl with a big bust. Get what I mean? The image that comes to mind is sort of a slutty type with teased hair and eye makeup up to here, kind of dumb, etc. Without claiming any ability to be objective, I do not think I am that type. Also, the boys that are attracted to girls with big busts, are the bottom of the barrel, in my opinion. Sort of sleazy, dumb, awful guys.

This is not a problem I can discuss with Mom since, as I mentioned, she has no bust at all and has gone without a bra without anyone noticing for the last two years. If I went without a bra, it would be a major catastrophe. I can't discuss it with Oliver because he thinks it's very funny and thinks the expression "C cup" is hilarious. Much he knows.

However, apart from these melancholy reflections about myself, I felt, looking out over the room, that we had done very well.

Each of the tables had a small vase of fresh wild flowers picked by Oliver and me that very morning. I much prefer wild flowers to roses and the like. They looked very gay and rustic. There was a single white candle on each table which did make the light soft and appealing. Ralph had something there. Everyone exclaimed over the food, though of course since they were parents or friends of parents this was not a good test. I helped bone several trout. The trick is to get the whole bone out without flaking up the fish. Letty and Joyce looked pretty in black skirts and shocking pink blouses. At first, as I had expected, Joyce thought it was unfair I should have such an easy deal, being *maitre d'hotel* while they were waitresses, but she finally piped down. I think basically she is glad to have the job. Now she can see Oliver (whom she's always had a crush on) more.

Oliver was quite busy in the kitchen, fretting over his trouts and steaks. In fact, everything was so well organized ahead of time that there was not an inordinate amount to do. However, Oliver was sweating and looking worried and Sara Lee was hanging over him, handing him lemons and parsley as though they were doing an open heart operation. I guess it is good to take your work seriously. Melrose Pfeifer, who was sitting with Mom, exclaimed over Oliver's talents as a chef. Mom said, "Oh, he's been making his own food since he was two. He made cream puffs when he was six."

Luckily Oliver was in the kitchen and could not hear all this. Melrose Pfeifer said, "You certainly have a very talented family," and Mom kind of grinned and said, "Yeah, they're okay."

"Will Daniel be visiting the restaurant?" I heard him say. Luckily, being *maitre d'hotel* on a slow night (I hoped this was a slow night and not a typical night) gives you an excellent chance to eavesdrop.

"Who knows?" Mom said.

"He is, you think—" Melrose started to say when

Mom said, "Let's not get into a big thing about marriage, Mel, okay?"

I don't know if Melrose Pfeifer had intended to "get into a big thing about marriage," whatever that means, but he just looked startled for a moment and then reached over and patted Mom's hand, looking or trying to look "understanding" and said, "Sure, Vera. I know exactly how you feel."

The next night was an utter flop. We had one couple all evening! They were a very nice couple with a baby in a basket. I knew Oliver would say babies were forbidden, but it was ten o'clock on a Saturday night and we had all been standing morosely around doing nothing for two hours. Sara Lee was reading Tolkien aloud to Oliver in the kitchen, Henry and Zachary were playing gin rummy, and I was wishing I had brought my cello so I could at least practice the Telemann trio we had decided to do for the first chamber music night. The couple with the baby were fine. I'm not the type who thinks all babies are cute, but this baby was a very nice person—very quiet and well behaved. It sat there in its infant seat and waved a rattle around, looked appreciatively at Mom's paintings, and even sucked on a crust of French bread (flown over from France that very day, according to the bag it came in). I wish more people were that polite. I had been afraid the couple would think eight dollars a dinner was a bit steep since I gather couples with babies are usually short of money, but this couple just smiled and ate and didn't seem to notice or care that they were the only people present. It was certainly quiet, you can say that. Lugubrious might be a better word.

Sunday night was a little better. The Effings showed up. They were both very bouncy types who kept saying how marvelous everything was even before they'd eaten a mouthful. After the meal they came into the kitchen to "congratulate the chef."

"You've got to give me that recipe for lemon chicken," Mrs. Effing shrieked, seizing Oliver like a hawk with a mouse. "It's the most marvelous thing I've ever eaten! Wasn't it, Myer?"

"Superb," Mr. Effing said. "Young man, you have a great future ahead of you."

I doubt very much that Oliver intends to be a chef, but he looked pleased anyway and gave forth with various self-deprecating mumblings.

"We're going to tell everyone we know about this place," said Mrs. Effing. "You children are just marvelous! I can't get over it."

I hope Mrs. Effing has a lot of friends. Unfortunately, she is the type that makes it hard to tell how sincere she is. Still, even if she tells a few people, it will be better than nothing.

Monday was a slight improvement, though we weren't sure why. It still wasn't even half of capacity, but we were beginning to be grateful for anything. Ralph kept saying we shouldn't judge, that the first week was nothing. He said it would take at least a month to tell if we were going to make it. Luckily, we had not invested much since the Stollingwells had enough plates and silverware. Oliver would have liked to use much fancier stuff, but Ralph and I had restrained him. I guess if you are going to have a restaurant that will be open all year it's one thing. Anyway, with the candlelight I bet not many people could tell the difference.

Late Monday night Oliver and I called Dad. We were on different extensions. While the phone was ringing, I said, "Ol?"

"Yeah—what?"

"Hi!"

"Hi to you."

"Do you think he's there?"

"We shall see."

On about the tenth ring Dad answered the phone.

"Dad? Hi, it's us, we're on different extensions."

"Oh, hi kids! Hey, isn't this a little late?" It was eleven-twenty.

"No, we have to stay up late to clean up after the restaurant," I said.

"Oh, say, I heard about that. It sounds terrific. How's it going?"

"Pretty well," Oliver said.

"Very well," I said. "Oliver's lemon chicken was deemed superb by an old-time gourmet."

"Oliver's lemon chicken *is* superb," Dad said.

"Listen, the reason we called," I said, "is that we have to go into the city to get some stuff for the restaurant and we thought we might drop over . . . or stay over actually."

"Which will it be—drop over or stay over?"

"Stay over, I guess," I said, "if you can put us up. We can bring sleeping bags."

"Oh, that won't be necessary," he said. "Well, great. When will it be?"

"Is tomorrow too soon?" I said.

"Couldn't be better."

He was certainly in a genial frame of mind. Wish I could say the same for Mom. Anyhow, we planned the details and hung up.

"Well, at least now we'll find out about the girl friend bit," I said to Oliver while he was brushing his teeth. I always feel I have a captive audience while Ol is brushing his teeth since he can't talk back that well.

"Car, come on ... you've got to stop all this snooping-around stuff."

"I'm not! Did I say anything about snooping? I'm just going to get a feel of things, that's all. And I wish you would too."

"I believe in privacy," Oliver said. He took a mouthful of water and rinsed. Oliver used to use a water pik and that really was quite a production. It's enough of a production anyway. He spends about an hour going over his teeth with dental floss. Ironically, he has lousy teeth and I don't have even one filling. I had one in a baby tooth but it fell out.

"Oliver, you know you are a—"

"Are you two still up?" It was Mom. She was in her red and white one-piece pajamas with the feet—the type that nine-month-old babies wear with a flap for the behind in back. I have never been certain of the origin of those pajamas of hers.

"Just turning in," I muttered and raced off to bed. I didn't want Mom to know about my speculations on Dad's doings. Maybe she knew?

New York is not a bad place. I miss it at times. We lived there till Oliver and I were eight. Then Dad got this counseling job and we had to move. I know there's supposed to be mugging and stuff, but nothing like that ever happened to me except once. That once was on a summer day when I'd just bought an ice cream. I was holding my purse and someone came up behind me, snatched it, and ran away. The funny part was that I had no money in my purse. None at all. I'd just spent my last dime on the ice cream. So I turned around and yelled, "But it has no money in it!" Then I realized that was pretty silly. I mean, by then the guy had run clear around the block anyway. And it wasn't as though he would have turned around, come back with the purse, and said, "Sorry. I'll try someone with more cash on them." It wasn't even a good purse, actually, just a cheesy Woolworth's one. I figured it served him right.

When I think of New York, I remember the nice things like bicycling with Oliver in Central Park on Saturday afternoons. Also, ice skating in Wollman Memorial and seeing movies on Sunday night with Mom and Dad and having pizza afterward at V and T's. They had great pizza. I also remember this one vignette I saw when I was walking our dog in the park. I passed a park bench and on it sat a basset hound, a black man playing a saxophone, and a little old lady reading a newspaper. They were sitting there about equally spaced from each other, the basset hound and the little old lady on each end, the black man in the middle. You couldn't tell who belonged to who. I always think of that when I think of New York.

Dad, as I believe I mentioned, has sublet an apartment on East Seventy-Eighth Street. Oliver and I had quite a few errands to do and we didn't get there till nearly dinner time on Tuesday. We were fairly laden down with spices, *madeleine* pans from Bloomingdales, and other purchases for the restaurant.

"Hi, kids!" Dad said. He had grown a beard.

I hate it when men grow beards. It's bad enough on guys Ralph's age. It's just plain awful on someone Dad's age.

"How do you like it?" Dad said, evidently seeing me watching him critically.

"Is it a permanent growth?" I asked.

"It could be," he said.

I sighed. "Yeah, it's—" I muttered something and then said I had to wash up.

The trouble is that Dad thinks I am too critical. So I hate to give him ammunition for this belief which may well be true. I think the problem is this: I think Dad would like me to be the kind of daughter that hangs on his every word and thinks he is the greatest thing that ever lived or breathed. This, however, is just not my personality. I like many people, even love a good many, but I guess I don't "revere" that many. I hope if I ever get married, I marry someone who does not mind this.

I think Dad minds it more now that I am an adolescent and have breasts and all that. I once read this play in which a father who has many affairs tells his daughter that the reason he had them was because she was always too cold to him. He said that an admiring daughter would make a father feel so good he would not need or want to have affairs. This may well be a canard. I do not put that much stock in plays. However, I certainly hope it will not be true of our family. I do love Dad very much. I just do not think he is uttering God's truth every time he opens his mouth.

We chatted a bit about the restaurant. Then Dad said, "Speaking of food—there's a great pizza place down the block. I thought I might go down for one. What do you say?"

"Sounds okay to me," I said. Then I looked at Oliver. I know Oliver had been hoping Dad would take us to some big deal French restaurant so he could compare his watercress soup to theirs and all that. But the trouble is, I don't think Dad would spend that much money on us, as I told Oliver on the train. He really doesn't think of us as grown-up enough. Also, Dad is not that much of a gourmet himself and it might just never occur to him.

"We can go out, of course," Dad said.

"Actually, I'm a bit tired," I said. Which was true. We'd been walking all day and it was hot as a beast out. Dad's sublet apartment was wonderfully air-conditioned. I just felt like plopping down on a sofa and going to sleep.

Oliver said pizza would be okay. I felt sorry for him, he looked so downcast.

While Dad was out, I began snooping around the apartment. I wasn't snooping, really, just taking it all in, as they say. Frankly, I think it was a very ugly apartment. Not that Dad was responsible, but I had the feeling he thought it was great. Everything was white vinyl or chrome or glass. The windows were all sealed. It just had a very airless look to it. Still, I guess if you're a family man and you've always had to buy old tweedy furniture so your kids won't scuff it, maybe it's nice to be surrounded by all this white stuff. Even the carpet which was wall-to-wall was white. In the bedroom was a huge bed, and on one wall was a wall system with everything built in including a TV, hi-fi set, and all that. There was a digital clock on the night table. I don't know. To me it just looked like some bachelor's den out of *Playboy* magazine. There was nothing original about it. If this was Dad's taste, it didn't say much for it.

"How do you like it?" I said to Oliver who was lying on the sofa reading *The New York Times* food page.

"What?"

"The place . . . the way it's done."

"It's okay."

"It gives me this very spooky feeling," I said.

"Oh come on," Oliver said.

"No, I mean it. Doesn't it to you?"

"Well, the couch is extremely comfortable."

"The bed is big enough for eight," I said grumpily. I wish I could get Oliver to criticize things once in a while.

"Maybe he has orgies here."

"Wow!" I said with mock excitement. I slumped into a chair. Oliver was right. The furniture was extremely comfortable. I took off my shoes and wiggled my feet in the rug. It was about four inches thick. There were certainly enough creature comforts about, I'll say that.

Dad came back bearing a huge pizza, some beer, and some cokes. We ate in the living room at the glass coffee table.

"How do you like my place?" Dad said, kind of smiling in this way that confirmed my belief that he thought it was great.

"It's nice," I said, but couldn't resist muttering, "if you like that kind of thing."

Dad just looked at me.

"That bed is quite something," I said. "Do you sleep eight across or what?"

Dad laughed. "That bed is really two beds," he said, "side by side, self-righteous young lady."

I wonder if I really am a self-righteous young lady. The only thing which would make me think that this is not just Dad's opinion is a time at school that I had a talk with the school principal, Dr. Brown. It was because I had started a petition to get the art teacher fired. She was really lousy, but it turned out she could not be fired because she had tenure. I guess tenure is good for the teachers, but it's not so good if, in a subject you like, you get stuck with some idiot year after year. This was the case with art in our school. However, Dr. Brown said that the staff had discussed me and that they had come to the conclusion that I was someone who set very high standards for myself and other people. "You may live up to them," he said, "but not everyone else can." It seemed a polite way of calling me a pig-headed fool. Oddly, I had never thought of myself as striking people this way, but perhaps I do. In this particular case, I did not mean that it would be bad for Dad to have orgies of eight people in the bed, though perhaps my tone led him to believe that.

"How is your mother?" Dad asked. He was not eating any pizza, just drinking some beer.

"As well as can be expected," I said.

He nodded. What does he mean "your mother"? Isn't she his wife? I mean, he must talk to her on the phone at least.

When we were finishing up, Dad said, looking a little embarrassed, "Kids, the thing is—I've got to go out for just a couple of hours—I'm really sorry. Something just came up. Will you be okay? The building's very well guarded, but if you—"

"We'll be fine," Oliver muttered. I guess he still hadn't gotten over Dad's not taking us out to a fancy place.

"I'll try not to be back too late," he said, "but, if you want to go to sleep before I get back, why don't you sleep on the two beds?"

"Where will you sleep?" I asked.

"The couch converts to a bed," Dad said.

Shortly after this he left.

Oliver went into the bedroom, stretched out with his shoes off, and began watching a movie called "Wingless Victory." There are some movies that I know right away I will not like. Movies with names like "Wingless Victory" are one of them. I could not say what that movie would be about, but I sensed it was not my type of thing.

I began to wander around the apartment. It was so neat there was not much you could do. I hadn't really—honest!—intended to snoop. I sat down at the big walnut desk and began looking in the drawers thinking I might find some paper and pencils so I could draw a little. Instead I found Dad's novel.

I must confess I read it.

Dad has been talking about writing a novel ever since I can remember. Every summer he closets himself in the den and tries to work on it. The trouble is, working on it or not working on it seems to make his blood pressure go up. Then he has to stop and go out and play tennis so it will go down again. The trouble with tennis is that his blood pressure mostly goes down if he wins, but lately Ralph has been beating him so frequently that he finally told Dad he didn't think it would be fair for them to play singles anyway. That made Dad feel great, naturally.

What can I say? I didn't think the novel was good. And not thinking it was good made me feel awful. I wanted so much either to like it or think it was good. I guess those aren't always the same.

I mean, sometimes I like books—mysteries, for instance—that I know aren't good, and sometimes I know a book is good, like Moby Dick, but I don't much enjoy reading it.

It was a war novel. I guess I have always felt—what can you say in a war novel? Can you say, "War is great, I loved every minute of it, nothing gave me a greater thrill than seeing all that blood and gore and poor people suffering. I hope there'll be bigger and better wars in the future?" No, you can not. Or at least the war novels I have read do not. They usually take a fairly standard pacifist position. Which is fine by me, I'm a pacifist myself, but it's just not that interesting.

After I had finished it, I sat for a long time biting my nails and thinking gloomy thoughts. I wanted to tell Oliver I'd read it, but I knew he would say that had been snooping and a terrible thing to do. So I just wandered around the apartment some more. Finally I went into the bedroom and said, "Hey, guess what? I just read Dad's novel."

Oliver's eyes didn't even flick from the TV screen. "Umm?"

"Aren't you even curious how it was?"

"Was it moderately lousy or extremely lousy?" Oliver said.

"Ol, you are a—. How did you know it would be lousy?"

"What did you—expect it to be good?"

I sat down on the edge of the bed. "Sure, why not?" I said.

He just looked at me.

"Well, I didn't really *expect* it to be good," I clarified. "I just kind of hoped."

Oliver kept watching the movie. He said, "Boy, I really pity the person who marries you."

"Why?"

"You are such a sneak. I've never seen anything like it."

I felt my face grow hot. "Look, I wasn't planning to read it—I just came upon it."

"Sure."

"Well," I said. "I pity the person who marries *you*. You're just a fat-headed prig!"

With that I stormed off into the bathroom and took a bath.

It was a wonderful bath.

You may not be aware of this, but the best way to feel good on a very hot day is to take a very hot bath. As hot as you can stand. Then, when you come out, especially if there's air conditioning, you feel freezing. I made the water so hot I began turning red. I even washed my hair under the faucet. When I came out, clad in my pajamas, I felt very peaceful and serene.

Oliver was in his pajamas. "Let's turn in," he said.

"Okay," I said.

Just as I was climbing into bed, the phone rang. It was on my side so I answered it. It was a girl. She seemed a little startled to hear my voice. She said, "Is this TR7-6132?"

"Yes," I said.

"Is—a—Daniel there?"

"No, he's gone down for a few hours," I said.

"May I take a message?" I've gotten pretty good at this since I became *maitre d'hotel*.

"Well, could you—a—maybe you could just tell him Frances called."

"Sure," I said.

"Who was that?" Oliver wanted to know.

"Some person," I said. I clicked off the light.

Oliver went right to sleep; he always does. I could not sleep. First I was bothered by the digital clock. I don't mind an ordinary ticking clock because that's at least a steady sound you can get used to. But this way there'd be silence and suddenly this flicking sound. The first few times I'd jump up, thinking a pencil had rolled off the night table or there was a mouse in the closet. Finally, I said, "Hey, Ol, do you mind if I unplug the digital clock?"

He just kind of mumbled so I unplugged it, wrapped it in a towel, and put it in a drawer.

I still couldn't get to sleep.

I decided to make myself a cup of cocoa. I padded into the kitchen quietly—not that it would matter, Oliver sleeps like a rock—and opened the refrigerator door. You may not believe this, but it was empty, except for one can of sardines and a bottle of vodka. Can you imagine? A whole huge refrigerator even bigger than the one we have at home with nothing in it? Even more amazing was that all the cupboards were empty too. I mean, maybe men living alone don't cook that much, but a house without even some cocoa or crackers is in a pretty bad way. Being desperate, I went into the living room and foraged around in the pizza box which still had a few old crusts in it. They were not bad.

Back in bed, I just sat there. I once read in a book the expression "awash with sadness." That was exactly how I felt. I literally felt I was lying on a beach and big waves of sadness were coming along and knocking me over every time I tried to sit up.

I kept thinking of this one thing which to me would be the most depressing thing I could imagine. I once knew this girl whose father remarried. He married this young girl about five years older than his daughter and they had a new family together. On holidays and stuff, the father would bring these little tiny kids over to my friend's house. Anyway, I kept imagining this would happen with Dad. I think I could survive Dad's remarrying, maybe, but the thought of those tiny little kids was more than I could take. It didn't seem fair.

I know I am leaping to conclusions. Dad is not yet remarried or even thinking about it for all I know. Even if he did remarry, he might not want to have more children at all. There's the money to consider, for one thing. Oddly, that point, practical as it was, cheered me up. Dad just couldn't afford more children. It was as simple as that.

On that note I fell asleep.

In the morning Dad took us out for breakfast. He took us to a really nice place with fat grandma-like waitresses, and they had perfect poached eggs, real country ham, and delicious hot chocolate with whipped cream on top. I am glad there is always food to turn to. It really is a big consolation. Without food I would be in a bad way.

"By the way, Frances called last night," I said.

Dad blushed. This is a funny thing about Dad. He must be one of the few men in his forties who actually blush. It's quite sweet in a way. "Oh, well ... fine," he said. "Thanks for taking the message, Car."

"Dad, will you come to our restaurant?" Oliver said. "It's really good. You should."

"Of course I'll come!" Dad said. He looked so enthusiastic I practically forgave him for everything.

"We're closed Tuesday and Wednesday," I said.

"Maybe this Saturday," he said.

Then we told him a bit more about it, about chamber music night and all that. He said he might try to come for one of those nights too.

Chapter Eight ☘ The Fall of Oliver, the Rise of Letty

I am beginning to like Letty Pfeifer. I guess I had always lumped her together with Joyce, which is wrong. They are very different. Every afternoon this week, Oliver, Letty, and I have practiced our trio out in the back of the Stollingwells' under the oak tree. We meet from two to four. It is always very quiet then with a wonderful piney smell in the air. There are wild flowers all over the place. Playing out of doors is very nice.

Letty is very good at the viola. I would almost go so far as to say she is better than I am at the cello, but it is hard to make direct comparisons. In any case, it is clear she takes it very seriously. We are rehearsing a Telemann trio. Oliver sits leaning against the tree, Letty stands with her viola, and I sit on a folding chair. We sounded very good.

At one point when we were taking a break and drinking lemonade, Letty suddenly said, "I wish my mother could come and hear us play."

She began to talk about her mother. It seems I did not quite have the right story about Letty's mother. I never knew, for instance, that she was a really good artist and has even had one-man shows in New York. I thought she had always been crazy and in mental hospitals, but Letty said that up 'till now she was never in for more than six months at most. She said that when her mother is at home she is mostly like anyone else. Only she will get very quiet and suddenly go off for walks by herself. You could tell from the way Letty talked about her that she was very fond of her mother. When Joyce would talk about Letty's mother, it was always with a kind of contempt, so I had thought she was probably some real looney who thought she was a ghost of Abraham Lincoln or something.

Letty has red hair and a lot of freckles now that it is summer. Her nose is quite big, which is why I guess you could not call her pretty. She also has quite big hands for a girl. When she talks, she doesn't quite look at you but looks to one side or at the ground. But when she talked to Oliver and me about her mother, she looked right at us with her greenish eyes.

I could tell Oliver liked her. He said, "Why don't we write your mother and ask her to come? She might like an invitation."

"That's a nice idea," Letty said, but in sort of a sad way. I had the feeling she didn't think her mother would come.

I have noticed that after the restaurant closes and we set off for home, Oliver has been walking Letty home. Just Letty, not Joyce. Still, it was a bit of a shock when one night, as I was fiddling around, getting ready to go to sleep, he came into my room and said, "Car? Listen, where do you draw the line?"

I looked up, startled. "Huh?"

Oliver looked terribly embarrassed. "I mean, like, with a boy, what do you think is okay for a boy to do and what isn't? I realize this is sort of a personal issue, but—"

I thought a minute. I really wasn't thinking so much of what he had asked as of the oddness of Oliver asking. As I say, until this moment I had always assumed Oliver would a) never be an adolescent, b) never get married. I guess I am not always right. "I guess anything above the belt is pretty much okay," I said.

"Above the belt," he said, musing. "Is this ... I mean, is this based on personal experience or just abstract reasoning?"

"A touch of each," I said.

Oliver sat down under the window sill, his knees up to his chin. I went and closed the door. Mom's room is around the corner and I don't think she is usually an eavesdropper, like some I could mention, namely me, but I thought it wise to be on the safe side.

"So you and Letty are really making it, eh?" I said, sort of joking around. Actually, I felt kind of sad. When I had thought earlier this summer that Oliver and I were coming to the parting of the ways, I guess I just had never imagined anything like this. If anything, I imagined I would be the one to get interested in boys and sex and so forth before he would. It was extremely depressing. I guess all these years I had always thought of Oliver and me as a team in the way Ralph and Sara Lee are and Mom and Dad were. Probably what I was hoping, though I never really thought it out, was that this would last until I found somebody I liked. Live and learn.

Also, I like Letty. She is really a nice person. For some reason this makes it worse.

"You're lucky," I said. "I wish I had someone."

"Henry likes you," Oliver said.

"Yeah ..." I realize this is true. Henry is not bad. He is tall and thin with what I guess could be called an impish expression and straight black hair like Sara Lee's. But somehow he does not turn me on. I could say he is not my type, but I am not sure I know what my type is. Sometimes I wonder how anyone gets to like anyone. I mean, if you rule out all the people who would never like you because they wouldn't like your looks or would be interested in different things, and then if you rule out people you might like but they live in Borneo and you live in Massachusetts, and if you rule out people you might have liked except they lived three hundred years ago, and then if on top of that you rule out people like Henry Takami when you have nothing against them or nothing for them, you wonder who is left. Sometimes I wonder how the world manages to go 'round. But I guess it does.

"Car?" Oliver asked suddenly.

"Umm."

"How old do you think we'll be when we sleep with someone?"

As it happens, this is not a subject which has never entered my head. I would say I have given it considerable thought. "I'd imagine sixteen or so," I said.

71

"Sixteen!" Oliver looked as though I had said he was going to be inducted into the army the next day. "That's in just a year and a half."

"Oh sure, only I don't mean the day you hit sixteen you race into the street and grab the first person you see. I just mean roughly sixteen—let's say sixteen to eighteen. How's that?"

Oliver looked very relieved. "I don't think I'm going to be ready at sixteen," he said.

Famous last words. He'll probably be doing it while I'm still sitting here cleaning out my bureau drawers. I'm getting suspicious of Oliver. "I'll probably be ready when I'm eighty," I said morosely. What happens if you're ready, whatever that means, and there's no person?

"When did Sara Lee and Ralph start sleeping together?" Oliver said.

"When they were eight," I said.

We both laughed. Then Oliver said, "Actually, I remember when they were both in the third year of high school Ralph told me they'd decided to stop because it was too emotionally exhausting."

"Hmm," I said. "Interesting. I presume they've resumed by now, however."

"I should think so."

At times I have envied Ralph and Sara Lee. Not many people know who they are in love with starting in third grade and really stick to that. The only thing is, you wonder if they won't be sick of each other after a while. So far, I must admit, this does not seem to have happened.

"Listen, Ol?" I said. "Let's tell each other when

we do it, okay? I think it would be very interesting to get an opinion from someone of the opposite sex."

"Yeah, sure, that sounds like a good idea," he said. He began fiddling with a pencil on the rug. "I feel sorry about Letty's mother," he said.

"That is too bad," I said.

"Letty says her mother really hates living here. She hates small-town life. She grew up in San Francisco."

"I think the best would be to live six months in each place," I said. "Six months in a city and six months in the country."

Oliver didn't look like he heard me. He said, "Letty thinks her father sort of likes Mom."

"Yeah, that figures," I said.

"What do you mean?"

"Well, he always looks at her with this kind of mournful expression."

"Maybe he's just horny."

We both laughed. "I shouldn't doubt it."

"So, what do you think will happen?" Oliver said.

"Search me."

But suddenly I got that "awash with sadness" feeling again. Boy, talk about moods! I'm really getting to be an expert. After Oliver left, I just sat and mooched around. I couldn't get to sleep and finally, at twelve or so, I went down to the kitchen to get a snack.

Everyone was up. Oliver was in the kitchen making watercress soup, Ralph and Sara Lee were playing chess in the living room, and Mom was just lugging a load of laundry up from the base-ment. Mom, which is very nice of her and quite unexpected, takes home all the tablecloths and napkins from our restaurant every night and washes and irons them. She is an excellent ironer.

"What are you doing up?" she said when she saw me.

"Everyone's up," I said.

"This is the summer of our discontent," Mom said and began folding tablecloths while seated at the bottom of the stairs.

"How come you're making soup?" I said to Oliver. "It's not soup day."

"I want to iron some kinks out of my watercress soup," Oliver said.

"Your watercress soup is great!" I said.

"Julia Child worked two years on a recipe for chocolate cake," Oliver said.

When Oliver is in that kind of mood, you can-not say much. As Royal Guinea Pig, I had a bowl of the soup which tasted exactly like his regular watercress soup. I also had a green apple, which I like to eat with lemon juice squeezed over it. It's so sharp it makes your teeth get a funny feeling, but I like it. I finished off with a few Oreos and trekked back to bed.

Sara Lee always beats Ralph at chess. He doesn't seem to mind.

Chapter Nine ❧ Dad Visits the Restaurant

The restaurant is doing well. Ralph seems to have been right. The first month you have to just kind of get the show on the road. By now I guess enough people have heard of us so that we rarely have a really bad night. Even on days like Monday and Thursday. Sometimes the same people come back. The couple with the baby came back. The baby was not quite as great as the first time. They said he was teething. Maybe that explains it. In any case, when they left, Oliver said no more babies. I knew he would say that. Now that we are getting pretty filled up, he feels we can be more choosy. It's not for him, he says. Most people do not want to eat next to a teething baby whether he is cute or not. Oliver may have a point.

We have had a few disasters.

Once Zachary spilled a whole sauce dish of *Béarnaise* sauce over a lady's lap. He is kind of a jerk. Henry, no matter what you say for him, is very good as a waiter, very diplomatic. After that incident, Ralph said Zachary had to be just a bus boy, namely, clear things and pour ice water for people. Zachary looked kind of disgruntled, but agreed.

One night Joyce claimed that a man had just propositioned her. I was standing at the back and she came up to me and pointed him out. Joyce is the type to make a big deal out of almost anything. It turned out that the man, who was there with his wife and said all this in front of her, had just said he thought she was an excellent waitress and, if she ever wanted, she could come work in their home. "You can have your own little room and your own little dog," he said. Joyce happens to have almost a phobia about dogs, as I recall from when they lived near us. Even a dachshund makes her cower. So the "proposition," such as it was, didn't go over too well.

I told her to cool it. "Men do that sort of thing," I said.

"How do *you* know?" she said sort of snottily. I think her nose is out of joint from Oliver's liking Letty.

"One learns," I said, smiling enigmatically. I know that kind of thing is terribly phony, but Joyce is such an ass.

Later in the evening, she came racing back to show me what a big tip the man had left for her. "That's an impressive tip," I said to soothe her feelings. "Hey Henry, did you know Joyce got a five-dollar tip?"

"What did she do to get it?" he said.

I laughed. Poor Joyce. Maybe she makes everyone feel that way.

That Friday night the phone rang in the restaurant. I picked it up and said, "Chez Simon. May I help you?" like I always do.

"Carla? Is that you? Hi, it's Dad."

"Oh, Dad, hi! Gosh, how funny."

"I'm calling to make a reservation for tomorrow," he said, "for two. Can you put me down?"

"Sure. That's chamber music night."

"I know, that's why I picked it."

"Well, great. See you then."

I felt terribly excited about Dad's coming. We'd been rehearsing the Telemann trio all week and it was really good now, as good as it could be with us playing. I was glad he hadn't come at the beginning when we were a bit rusty.

I decided not to tell Mom he was coming, in case it made her feel funny. I just told Oliver. I was really curious who he would come with. This would be the real test.

At eight thirty Saturday in walked Dad. He did have a girl or woman with him. I showed them to the table, my heart beating like anything.

"Carla, this is Frances," Dad said. "She teaches at The Manhattan School of Music."

"I've heard so much about you," Frances said, smiling.

"Naturally I've told her what a marvelous cellist you are," said Dad.

I felt myself go red. "Well . . . hope you like it," I mumbled, snatched up the reserved card, and darted off to the table where I usually stand.

So that was Frances of the phone call. But here was the funny part—she wasn't the least bit pretty. Certainly not what you could call a hippie from any stretch of the imagination. For one thing she looked at least in her late twenties or maybe even thirties. Possibly younger than Mom but not by much. Also, she had this perfectly regular face, no really bad features but nothing special. Brown hair tied back in a bun. She wore glasses even, not the fancy violet-tinted granny kind that pretty girls wear to look exotic. Just plain old tortoise shells. She looked like she had worn them all her life since she was six or something. She was wearing just a dark blue dress and her legs were quite fat—you know, the kind that don't go in much at the ankle, but just keep on going straight up.

I felt awful. It sounds silly, but if I was going to hate her, it would have been so much easier if she had been a dyed blond with jangly earrings and blue eye shadow. I mean, I hated her anyway, but I couldn't point to any really good reason for doing so.

What an odd person to pick. She wasn't even prettier than Mom or that much younger or *anything*.

When Letty passed by, I said, "That's my father."

"Oh, is that him? He's very nice-looking."

"Yeah, I guess."

"He looks sort of like that French writer, you know the one I mean, Camus."

"Yeah, kind of."

"Who's that girl with him?"

"I don't know ... some girl. Listen, Letty, could you do me this one favor?"

"Sure."

"When you wait on them, could you tell me

what they're talking about? I'd just be kind of curious."

"Oh sure." Letty rushed off. A minute later she came back. "Well, I can tell you what they ordered. He's having watercress soup, melon with prosciutto, and the steak rare; she's having mushroom broth, melon, and steak medium rare."

"Thanks, Letty."

I felt like an ass. Nonetheless, I kept staring at them all during the meal. They just seemed to be talking. I mean, they didn't hold hands or anything. It was hard to tell how close they were. Letty wasn't much help. I mean, she was nice, but the bits of conversation she reported were just ordinary things, nothing special.

At one point Henry came over and, giving me a grin, said, "I see your Dad is here with a cute chick."

I could have strangled him. He's so tactless and dumb. Sometimes I think it's true that boys my age are about ten years younger mentally than girls. "She's not exactly what you'd call a 'cute chick'," I said coldly.

You could tell he hadn't even looked at her, just wanted to be clever.

All during the trio I was very nervous. We played well and I don't think my nervousness showed, but my hands were sweating like anything and almost shook in the first movement. Luckily, by the third I felt better. Usually we play just one piece. If the crowd seems very enthusiastic, we sometimes play one movement again. Otherwise it's too tiring and goes on too long.

Frances and Dad came over afterward. "That was excellent," she said. She looked at me seriously. "How come you take the last movement so fast?" she said.

Most people don't even notice that. It was Oliver's idea, actually, and I'm not sure I've ever really agreed with him. He once heard a recording where it was done that way and liked the way it sounded. "Do you think it sounds too fast?" I said.

"No, It's just unusual. Harder to play, I would imagine."

"By now we're used to it," I said.

She was a hard person to hate. She looked so serious and bland, like one of those little girls who are always a little overweight in grade school and always last to be picked for games and stuff like that.

"How was your meal, Dad?" I said.

"Marvelous. Of course, I expected no less. No, I'm really impressed by you two. This is really a professional achievement."

Oliver came up and began talking to Dad and then Dad and Frances left.

Chapter Ten ⚡ What Happened on the Living Room Couch

That evening when we got home, we both went upstairs to our rooms. Mom was out. I believe she said she was going to a movie or something.

At around eleven I went down for a snack. I hope I'm not getting to be an insomniac, but lately I just don't fall right to sleep the way I used to. I find the best cure is a mug of hot milk with honey. We have these little jars of Trappist honey that someone gave Mom and Dad for Christmas. I've worked my way through the wild-flower honeys and am now up to orange blossom. They all taste pretty much the same.

On the way down the stairs, I glanced into the living room. I almost flipped. This is what I saw. Melrose Pfeifer was lying on the living room couch, his feet up on one end, his head resting in Mom's lap. He was lying on his back, staring at the ceiling, talking. Mom was sitting at one end of the couch, her legs straight out, her feet resting on a chair. She had a cigarette in one hand and a glass of what looked like sherry in the other. She was looking straight ahead with this kind of blank, dreamy expression. You couldn't tell if she was listening with rapture or not hearing a word he was saying. Anyway, luckily she didn't see me.

I raced up the stairs to Oliver's room. It was pitch black. "Hey, Ol—you've got to listen. You can't imagine what I saw downstairs on the living room couch."

"I'm asleep," he muttered.

"You are *not* asleep! How can you be if you just said, 'I'm asleep.'"

He said, "I was about to fall asleep before you—. So what'd you see? A black widow spider or what?"

"No, it's Mom and Melrose Pfeifer," I hissed.

"Look, close the door, will you? I can't hear if you whisper like that."

I closed the door. I sat down on the end of Oliver's bed. "It's Mom and Melrose Pfeifer—on the couch!" I said.

"So, what were they doing that was so unusual? What's the big deal?"

"They were just sitting there," I said weakly. Now that it came to it, I felt sort of an ass myself.

"Just sitting there! You mean, you come racing in here and wake me up just to say they were just sitting there?"

"Well, she's sitting, he's lying."

"And?"

"He's talking."

Oliver shook his head. "Gee, Car, this is really fascinating. I'm on the edge of my seat. Then what happened?"

I kind of laughed weakly. "You think there's nothing much to it, huh?"

"Well, nothing you've said so far amounts to

anything that I can see ... unless you left out some crucial fact—like they're both stark naked."

I gave out a whoop of laughter, then clapped my hand over my mouth.

We sat in silence a couple of minutes. "The thing is this, though," I said suddenly. "People should either get divorced when their children are little tiny babies or later when they're in college and married and stuff. Otherwise it's not fair."

"To who?"

"To the kids, of course!"

"Car, come on. Since when do people lead their lives like that?"

"Well, they *should*."

"Well, they *don't*."

I made a face. "I don't know, Ol—I just can't take any more of this."

"You! What have you been taking?"

"All this ... *stuff*," I grumbled. "All these comings and goings. All these different people—like that girl with Dad at the restaurant tonight."

"She looked like a perfectly harmless soul."

"I don't care," I growled. "I don't like it."

"Nobody likes it," Oliver said.

"So why is it happening?"

"These things just happen! People go through stages."

"At *forty*?"

"Sure! At eighty!"

I put my hands over my eyes. "Oh God, that's too depressing for words."

"Why, do you want your life to be all planned out at age twenty?"

83

"Yes!" I yelled.

"Well, you're in for a lot of surprises."

"Oliver, you are such a god damn ... realist! I hate you!"

"Will you let me go to sleep now?" Oliver yawned.

I sighed. "The thing is, I wanted a snack. That's why I started down the stairs to begin with."

"So, go get yourself a snack."

"What if I interrupt them or something?"

"Come on! Mom's probably out cold with boredom, listening to his life story or something."

"Yeah, I guess you're right." I got up reluctantly. "Sorry to have bothered you, Ol."

"Any time," he said.

I had the feeling he was sound asleep by the time I got to the door.

I stood at the top of the stairs, wondering if I should go down. Then I decided—the hell with it. I walked down very decisively, though my heart was beating like anything.

The living room was empty.

Mom was in the kitchen ironing tablecloths. "Oh, hi, Car," she said amiably. "Is it milk and honey time?"

"Seems to be," I said. I felt actually weak with relief and ambled over to the refrigerator. "I don't know, Mom, you know I just don't sleep the way I used to. I hope I'm not turning into an insomniac or something."

Mom folded one tablecloth and reached into the laundry basket for another. "You're just overtired, honey, really. Look at your face. You look like Humphrey Bogart or something. Look at those bags."

I went out into the hall and looked at myself. It was true. I had real bags, kind of greyish-looking. I always thought that was just an expression. I've read that these movie stars like Elizabeth Taylor say that they treasure every wrinkle or grey hair they get because it shows how much experience of life they've had and all that. But I think fourteen is a little young to be falling apart. I mean, like, I haven't even bloomed yet. If I ever will.

"You know, that restaurant is a very big responsibility for someone your age," Mom said. "It's great the way you and Ol are carrying it off; it's just that you have to take care of yourself."

"Sure, that's true," I said. I poured the milk into a saucepan and while it was heating dribbled in some honey right from the jar. "What movie did you see?" I asked.

Mom sneezed. "Oh, none, actually ... in the end. We just drove around." As I sat down at the kitchen table with my milk, she looked up and said, "Mel was telling me about his wife. It's so sad, really. Do you remember her from when they lived near us?"

I shook my head.

"She was such a lovely-looking woman," Mom said, ironing. "Sort of Indian-looking. . . . really black hair. The girls both look like Mel so it's hard to tell. But you know what I feel bad about? I used to think she was sort of cold and forbidding—I don't know, kind of contemptuous of all the 'just wives' around. She was a very good artist, you know, and really took it seriously. Anyhow, now Mel says she really was dying for someone to talk to but was just scared to make the overture. There were so many years I could have just gone over there for coffee or something!"

I gulped some of the milk. "Well, you never know at the time, I guess."

Mom reached for another tablecloth. "It's nice Oliver and Joyce are finally—"

"It's not Joyce, it's Letty," I said.

"Letty? I thought Joyce was the cute one."

"She is. Only Letty's the one Oliver likes."

"Really?" Mom frowned. "Are you sure? I think it's the other way around."

For some reason, that kind of thing just drives me up the wall. "Mom, I see these people every day. I ought to know."

"Umm." Mom looked abstracted. She didn't even hear what I said, I bet.

"Letty's the one who plays the viola with us," I added.

"Oh—the one with the nose, you mean?"

"Right, right."

Mom smiled. "Poor kid, getting a nose like that, just like Mel's. On him it looks okay."

"She's very nice, though," I said.

"Letty?"

"No, the man in the moon. Who were we talking about?"

At that Mom got a very hurt expression. I guess I should have apologized or said something, but it just kills me when she doesn't listen like that. She has this awful habit of jumping from one subject to another, and sometimes it seems like she doesn't listen to a thing.

I went back upstairs to bed, feeling sleepy. Ya, I know Mom is going through a lot. I should be nicer, I should be like Oliver. Well, I'm not. You are the way you are, right?

I just wish she would *listen* once in a while.

The week ended in a funny way.

Saturday evening when I went into the restaurant kitchen to give Oliver an order because Letty and Joyce were busy with something, I saw a most unfamiliar scene. Sara Lee was sitting on this high stool she usually sits on, kind of crying, and Oliver was patting her on the shoulder and saying something. When they saw me, they both looked up.

I felt awful. I didn't know what to say. "Umm— it's chicken and steak on that order, not chicken and trout," I said, just looking at Oliver. "That lady changed her mind."

"Okay," Oliver said.

I raced out of there. But for the rest of the evening I felt really funny.

Sara Lee just isn't the type to cry. If you saw Joyce crying, you'd know it could be anything, some really stupid little trivial thing. Some girls cry about anything. But Sara Lee is always so calm and soft. You would imagine something extremely bad would have to happen for her to be crying.

I wondered what it was. I also wondered if anyone else like maybe Letty, had seen her crying, but I didn't want to ask. Somehow because Letty is friendly with Oliver, I don't feel quite as close to her as I probably would otherwise. That's one disadvantage of having Marsha away this summer. She's just like me in loving to speculate about why things are happening. She'll be back fairly soon, in two weeks actually. It's amazing to think the summer's gone by so fast. I remember when she'd just left and I had just realized I wouldn't be going to camp and wondered how I'd survive the summer.

That evening I went into Oliver's room. This seems to be becoming a habit. As I say, maybe if Marsha was around, I wouldn't be doing it quite so much.

"How come Sara Lee was crying?" I asked.

Usually it's nice asking Oliver about things because he's so calm and unflappable. But this time he just sort of stood there, looking at me in a kind of worried way. I went over to him, stuck a finger in his ribs, and in this tough way we used to use when we were kidding around and pretending to be gangsters, I said, "Shoot, or I'll drill ya fulla holes."

Oliver backed away. He didn't even smile. "She's pregnant."

I looked at him, frowning. "How can she be pregnant?"

"How? What do you mean *how?*"

"I mean, like, isn't she on the pill or something?"

"I didn't ask," he said.

"Oh boy! You'd think she'd at least use—"

"Car, does it really matter all that much what she did or did not use? Suffice it to say that the methods employed, whatever they were, proved inadequate."

"Gotcha, son, gotcha." I leaned back, envisioning the whole thing. "You know, frankly, this is the dumbest thing I've ever heard of."

"Why dumb?"

I sat up again indignantly. "Well, my gosh! I mean, I can see, like, if you're in the back seat of a car and swept off your feet in passion—. But, I mean, they've been going together since they were in diapers practically."

"Ya, I know what you mean."

We just looked at each other. I was silent a moment. "I guess she feels pretty bad, huh?" I could understand Sara Lee picking Oliver to confide in; he is a good shoulder at such times.

"No, as a matter of fact, she's overjoyed—just tickled pink."

"What's going to happen, then?"

"She'll have an abortion, I guess."

"Done by who?"

"Well, as a matter of fact when you burst in on us this evening, I was just telling her ... there's this article in *Consumer Reports* I read a couple of months ago that—"

"Ol, you're great! Seriously, I knew you'd have read an article. I just *knew* it."

"Anyway, it tells the whole spiel and it's not that expensive—safe, recommended doctors, etc."

"Well, so it shouldn't be a trauma, anyway."

Oliver was standing there looking at me.

There's always something coming when he gets that expression. I steeled myself. "Yes?"

"You're not going to like this," Oliver said.

"Okay."

"It's just an idea I had."

By now I was just looking at him. "Shoot."

"Well, I was thinking we could pay for the abortion out of some of the proceeds from the restaurant." While I sat there, mouth hanging open, he went on, "We've netted over a thousand and, according to this article, it wouldn't cost more than a few hundred. So we'd still have a good profit and—I said you wouldn't like it."

"Have I said anything?"

"*Do* you like it?"

I sighed. "Oliver, we have worked the whole damn summer on this thing. I mean, you know, we've worked like *dogs*. Look at us! Everyone else is brown as berries and we look like ghosts. And you want to throw it all away just for—"

"It's a gesture," Oliver said. "She feels bad and I thought she would feel better to know we're behind her and sympathize and so on."

"Why can't Ralph pay? He could dig up the money."

"I know he could. Don't you see it's not a matter of that. It's a *gesture*."

I sat staring at the floor. "You're so altruistic."

Oliver said nothing.

"We won't do it if you don't agree," he said.

It was the situation with camp all over again. Oliver always paints me into these corners.

"Think it over, if you like," he said.

91

I sat there, thinking. You know, until this summer I always thought of myself as a fairly compassionate person. I realize self-deception is rife, but I didn't realize it was this rife. I guess Oliver made off with all the altruistic genes when our chromosomes were dividing.

"Sure, let's do it," I said finally.

Oliver smiled. "That's nice of you, Car."

"You were the one who thought of it."

"Yeah, but I can see how, being a girl, maybe you . . . . Well, anyhow—"

"Have you mentioned it to her yet?"

"Not yet. I thought I might tonight."

"You don't want to tell Ralph first?"

"We could. But I'd rather tell her first."

"Okay."

I got up and started to leave the room. Oliver said, "Hey, Car?"

"Umm?"

"Listen, I wouldn't . . . tell too many people. You know, like even Mom, I think—"

"Of course not!"

I stamped out of the room. I guess I should have felt all glowing with the thought of a good deed, but I still felt somehow mad and disgruntled. Maybe it was the fact that being a girl, this seemed more of a writing on the wall. And it's not that I have anything against abortion. I think it's fine. I'd do it myself—seriously. It's not that. I think it would be just plain dumb for them to have a kid now and mess up their lives. Sara Lee wants to be an architect and I know, I just know, if she had this kid, she never would—like a million other of those sad girls you see with teenage kids at twenty-eight. That must be just awful. So I really don't think I'm such a moralist. Maybe I'm just mean. Maybe I don't like someone else being the center all the time. It just seems this whole summer everyone is all full of these problems and I'm supposed to sit here and be so sympathetic just because, supposedly, my life is so calm and lovely and free from woe. That is mean, let's face it. I'm really a very mean person.

Chapter Twelve ❧ A Perfectly Simple Operation

That night at the restaurant, Oliver evidently told Sara Lee about our offer. When I went into the kitchen, she turned to me with this radiant smile and said, "I love your brother."

At first I thought she meant Ralph, but then I realized she meant Oliver.

"Ya, he is kind of nice," I muttered. I just couldn't pull it off with good grace. I raced out before she could thank me too.

I guess news travels fast because at around eleven-thirty Letty came over to me and hissed in my ear, "That's so nice—what you and Oliver are doing for Sara Lee."

"Oh—yeah," I hissed back.

"Most people just think of themselves in a thing like this," she said. "They don't even try to help the other guy." Her eyes were all shining too. Of course, she loves Oliver so maybe that's why.

"Letty, listen, one thing. Could you, um, not tell your father about this? I mean, it's just that we—"

She looked at me and laughed. "Are you kidding? Tell my father!"

"Well, you know. I didn't think you would, but it's good to be on the safe side."

About fifteen minutes later Henry sidled up and said, "I hear your brother knocked up my sister."

I hate that expression: knocked up. I mean, I know it's just a colloquial expression and shouldn't be taken literally, but it still bugs me. I just glared at him. Then I said, "Henry, listen, will you swear absolutely not to tell anyone—even your parents?"

"Even my parents! Why should I tell *them?*"

I guess nobody talks to their parents much. "No reason," I said. "Just ... well, you know, if you're not really careful, these things leak out and it would be better—"

"You really think I'm dumb, don't you, Carla?"

"Henry, I do *not* think you're dumb. I just mentioned it to you the way I mentioned it to Letty—to keep all outlets closed."

Ralph isn't always in the restaurant in the evening. So he wasn't informed until the next day. And not by us at all but by Sara Lee.

At around noon when Oliver and I were in the kitchen working on soups for the next week, he came in. "Hi, kids!"

"Hi, Ralph!"

He stood looking at us and smiling. "That was a nice idea you had but forget it."

"Why?" Typical of me. I'd hated the idea at first but now that I was getting used to it, I couldn't stand the idea that it might not go through.

"Because I can pay for this myself! Good Lord,

It certainly shows a funny picture of me that you two must have if you think I'd let you—"

"—foot the bill," I interjected.

"The point is, I have the money and I don't exactly appreciate the two of you meddling in my affairs!"

Talk about guilty consciences! "We were not meddling in your affairs!" I said.

"We wanted to make a gesture," Oliver said. I could tell he was mad too, but, as always, calmer than me.

"Okay, forget I said that," said Ralph. "I know you meant well."

"We knew you could raise the money," I said. "It wasn't a matter of that. We just thought Sara Lee felt bad and wanted to let her know we all—"

"Look, I know your motives were marvelous," Ralph said. "Okay? I realize that."

"Boy, what a family!" I said.

Oliver said, "Easy, Car." To Ralph he said, "When's she going to have it?"

"Tuesday probably."

"Next Tuesday?"

"Yeah. We called up. There doesn't seem to be any—"

"I've heard it's a perfectly simple operation," I said quickly.

"Oh sure," Ralph said. "There's nothing to worry about, really."

He still looked very uncomfortable in front of us. "Okay, so no hard feeelings, right? I just wanted to let you know how I feel."

"Perfectly okay," Oliver said.

It's funny. At times I think Oliver likes Ralph even less than me, but he would never say. We continued with our soup making, left alone in the kitchen.

"We are now richer than we were five minutes ago," I said.

"I could see his point," Oliver said.

"Oh, you can always see everyone's point!" I growled.

"I thought you'd be happy. Here you have the money and you get the credit for making the gesture."

"True." I wasn't sure why I still felt exactly the same, or if anything more mad. "It's just ... he hates to let us take part in anything. He was always like that! Remember when we were kids and he wouldn't even let us go into the living room if he was there with someone. He always has to have these private things."

"Well—" Oliver shrugged.

At that point Mom came into the room. She was in her chicken outfit, but just returning. She was holding the head part. "Umm—smells good," she said. "Can I taste?" She dipped a spoon into the soup. "Wow! Watercress soup just can't be this good," she said.

"The watercress is great this year," Oliver said, modestly.

"Jesus, that place was boiling," Mom said. She went to the refrigerator, took out the quart bottle of ice water, and began drinking it straight from the container. She drank several long gulps, put it back, and sat down. "They're supposed to have an air conditioner, but it was on the blink or something. I think my feathers were drooping."

I suddenly felt sorry for Mom. I have no idea why, out of the blue. She looked so silly in that chicken costume with her short hair all matted down. Seeing me look at her, she suddenly changed her expression. "Boy, this summer is a beaut, isn't it? I think it's gone on about eight hundred months. Maybe it's going to be summer the rest of our lives."

I began wondering what Mom would think about the thing with Ralph and Sara Lee. I mean, it's like I've said—you do and do not know your parents. I wouldn't imagine Mom would mind, but I'd be curious. Maybe she would. Would she be angry at Ralph?

"Car, stop staring at me," she said suddenly. "I know I look awful."

I snapped out of it. "No, it wasn't that."

The phone rang. Oliver went to answer it. He came back, saying, "It's Dad."

Mom got this funny expression on her face like someone had just socked her in the stomach. She went to the phone.

We couldn't really hear what she said. The phone is in the den and even though you can see it from the kitchen, you can't hear very well. My stomach began feeling funny. I went to the cupboard and took down the Pepto Bismol.

"What's wrong?" Oliver said.

"Too much soup, I guess," I said. I took a couple of swigs and put it back.

Chapter Thirteen ⚡ Blackberries

Oliver, Letty, and I were supposed to go pick blackberries that afternoon. They were all ripe and tasted marvelous. At first I thought I wouldn't go and then, at the last minute, I changed my mind. Picking blackberries can be good therapy. It's like painting a house. You do it and somehow your mind goes blank in a very peaceful way. I wore jeans and a long-sleeved sweat shirt since it can get pretty brambly. Letty even wears gloves, but I find that way I squash the berries and my hands get all sweaty.

It wasn't too hot when we got there. That is, the sun was strong, but in the shade it was quite cool. The blackberry bushes are in both the shade and the sun. They extend all the way in back of the lodge. We each had pails and began to pick. It was almost too easy. In the beginning of the season you had to pick very carefully, making sure you weren't getting any that were unripe. Blackberries are so sour that unless they're perfectly ripe they taste funny. Once a lady sent hers back because of that. But now the bushes were just laden with them. It was like clearing sand off a beach. You felt you could pick all day and night and there'd still be millions.

Usually I eat quite a few as I pick, but this time

I didn't feel too hungry. Maybe because of that, I filled the pail pretty quickly. I started in on another pail. I'd been picking in the sun and the top of my head felt hot. I decided to rest a little. I could've gone ahead to tell Letty and Oliver, but they were quite far down—I could just barely see them. Anyway, I knew they would pass by me on the way back. I went back to the oak tree, the one we usually practice under, and lay down. I fell asleep. I'm not usually a daytime sleeper. Oliver can just drop off anywhere, any time he wants, but not me. However, this time I was out cold in about one minute. Maybe it was all that insomnia or something. I slept very heavily, no dreams at all.

When I woke up, it was much cooler. It must have been nearly five o'clock. Oliver and Letty were sitting crosslegged right in front of me, the pails of blackberries next to them.

"Hey! How long have I been sleeping?" I asked.

"We don't know," Letty said. "We just finished picking." Her face was bright pink from the sun. She has that kind of fair skin that goes pink easily.

"Wow! I feel funny." I sat up and yawned. "I guess I was tired."

"You looked tired," Letty said in sort of a concerned way.

"I feel thirsty," I said.

"Oliver, why don't you go into the house and bring back a pail of water, okay?" Letty said. "I'd like some too."

Oliver went off toward the house.

Letty and I just sat there. It's such a beautiful setting, the Stollingwells' house. In winter it must be great all covered with snow. I don't think I've ever come here then. There's ice skating near by, but you can go another way, which we usually do.

"How has your mother been?" Letty said.

"Mom? Oh, okay, I guess."

I think another thing that has been at the back of my mind worrying me is this. Having Dad away all summer though odd and not nice, didn't seem so odd because the whole family is rarely together all summer. Either we're away or they sometimes take trips together, so it didn't seem too different from usual. Also, being busy with the restaurant had made me not think about it as much as I might have. But now, with the thought of fall coming and Dad not being here—it seemed like it would make much more of a gap. Also, it would make it seem more serious, being such a long time.

There's nothing I can do about it. I realize that. One girl I know whose parents separated actually called her father up or wrote him a letter or something, maybe both, saying, "Please come home," or that kind of thing. In a way I think that's terrible. Or maybe I'm just not the person to do it. Anyway, I'm not going to.

"Daddy said your mother is still in love with your father," said Letty.

"He did?" I got a kind of stomach cramp again. "Oh."

"Daddy's very fond of your mother, you know."

I just nodded.

"Do you think it's true?" Letty said.

"What?"

"About their still being in love."

"God, I don't know ... I mean, how could I know?"

"Well, if they weren't you might know."

"Would I? How?"

"I don't know," Letty said. "I think they would act differently."

I thought of this. "Maybe."

Oliver came back with the pail of water. We all had a few gulps.

"What are you looking so serious about?" he said.

"We were discussing love," I said. "No, it's just that Letty says her father says Mom and Dad are still in love and she wants to know if I agree. But I don't see how I can tell."

"Does he kiss her much?" Letty said. Then she blushed even pinker than she already was.

"Sometimes, I guess." It's funny how you don't really notice these things even though you'd think they were very important. Like not noticing if someone wears glasses even if you've known them all your life. "When they go on trips, I guess they do." I thought of this one picture in our family album of Mom and Dad standing in a field where he is standing in back of her with his arms around her. It's true that looks more passionate than the kind of thing they do now. That was before they

102

were married, I believe. "What do you think, Ol?" I said.

"I think they do," he said.

"Love each other or kiss each other?"

"Both. I mean, they're sort of modest about kissing probably. You know. I bet most people don't like to do that in front of their kids."

"Dad is much better-looking than Mom," I said, musing.

"No, he's not," Oliver said.

"Oh, Oliver, come on! You *know* he is!"

"I don't agree. Mom has a very beautiful, very unusual face."

I looked at Letty. "Oh, boy!"

Letty said, "In our family Mom is much better looking. But I'm not sure that matters so much. I mean, she doesn't seem to think she is."

"But, Ol, listen," I said. "Do you think they really, like, say 'I love you' and become passionate and that sort of thing when we're not there?"

"Sure."

I made a face. "I can't imagine it." I thought of the valentines Dad has gotten Mom over the years. It's true he always gets her one, never forgets, but they are more likely funny ones than really romantic ones. "The point is, can people really still *be* in love after twenty years?" I said.

"My grandparents were in love after sixty years," said Letty. "They really were. They did practically everything together. When he died, she died about four days later."

"Ya, I guess." You hear things like that, but it never seems that real.

103

"I would just *hate* to fall out of love right in the middle of being married," Letty said. "That must be the most awful thing that could happen."

"I may not even *get* married," I said. "That way you avoid the whole thing."

"Ya, but then you have other problems," Letty said.

"Like what?"

"You get lonely."

"You can visit people."

"Still."

"Well, anyhow," I said, "I'm certainly going to wait till I know every single thing about the person. I'm not going to just marry some person like that. I'll wait years and years till there's nothing I don't know."

Oliver snorted. "That sounds like you!"

I made a face at him. "Blah!"

Letty was looking from Oliver to me. "Did I tell you my mother's home?" she said.

So, that's what all this had been leading to! "No, that's great," I said. "When did she come?"

"Last week. She didn't want that many people to know at first. That's why I didn't mention it."

"How does she seem?" said Oliver.

"I think she seems good," Letty said. "In fact— well, you know, I was just wondering, would you like to come to my house to see her? I think she would like it."

"Really? Maybe she wouldn't," I said.

"No, she would. I've told her all about the restaurant and she really wants to meet you. She might even come some night, except she doesn't like crowds. Why don't you come?"

"Right now?" said Oliver.

"Sure—I'd invite you for dinner only—"

"Oh no," I said hastily. "Mom's expecting us."

We put all the blackberries in the refrigerator at the Stollingwells'. They keep very well. We could freeze them, but you can pick enough to last half a week easily.

Chapter Fourteen ⚡ Letty's Mother

We bicycled to Letty's house. It's further out of town than ours but is quite nice. It's made of grey stone. Letty said it was a very old house and that when they bought it they had to do a lot to make it work. It didn't have very good plumbing or anything like that.

When we got there it was very quiet and cool. All the curtains were drawn. Some people do that in the summer to make it cooler. We always forget and our living room can get boiling.

"She's probably in the basement," Letty said. "That's where she works."

We climbed down the stairs to the basement.

Letty's mother was sitting in a chair, sort of an old soft-looking armchair, biting her nails and looking at a picture that was up on an easel. I guess it was one she had made. I remembered Mom had said she looked Indian, but somehow I had taken that to mean American Indian with red-brown skin and high cheekbones, whereas she was more Hindu Indian with big black eyes and long black hair that was loose down her back. She was wearing these rather unusual colors—a pink blouse with bright purple cuffs, and dark red slacks. Somehow against the orange chair it looked like a picture itself.

"Mommy, this is Carla and Oliver."

"Hi, Carla and Oliver." Mrs. Pfeifer kept sitting on her chair. She didn't say, "I've heard so much about you," the way Mom might have, but she didn't seem sorry to see us either.

"These are some paintings Mom did," Letty said.

The whole basement which, like ours, was not fixed up nicely, had paintings everywhere. Some were hung, but most were just stacked up against each other or even lying on tables. We wandered around looking at them. They were interesting. I guess I had been afraid I would think they were really bad or just not my taste in some way. For some reason I'd been imagining they would be like those huge abstract paintings they show sometimes. But they were more sort of surrealistic. Like stretches of blue sky with a strange metal foot sticking out. She painted very well. I mean, it wasn't the kind of thing about which you'd say, "I could do that myself." The metal looked very real, as though you could touch it.

"Why do you use sky for a background so much?" Oliver said.

I was afraid she might get mad or think that was none of his business, but she said thoughtfully, "I don't know really.... There's something about sky and chrome that appeals to me right now. Chrome is so sensual in a way.... Anyway, I feel I've got to get it out of my system." She laughed.

We all went upstairs and had cokes.

"Would you like a drink? Some sherry?" she said.

It was funny. I wonder what made her think we would drink. In a way it was nice, treating us like adults. She made herself a drink and had it while we sat there. Letty was very quiet. She'd hardly said a word since we walked in. Maybe she was too nervous about the impression her mother might be making. Actually, I must admit that all the time we were there, I kept thinking of her being in these mental hospitals. But she didn't seem that different from anyone else. There was just one thing. Sometimes she would say something and then even if you were answering, she'd keep on talking so you found you were both talking on top of each other, sort of. I noticed that happened with me several times, but it happened with Oliver too. The other thing was that sometimes, for no special reason that you could tell, her eyes would suddenly expand a little, sort of like when you shine a flashlight in a dog's eyes. It made her look frightened. Then she would look just normal again.

"Tell Vera to give me a call sometime," she said. "I'd love to see her."

Vera means Mom. "We will," I said.

"How's her painting coming?"

"Oh, she doesn't do much really," I said. I was going to explain about Mom's being a chicken once a week and Dad and then it all seemed too complicated so I didn't say anything.

"She has a lot of talent," Mrs. Pfeifer said. "I love her sense of color."

Bicycling home, we didn't talk. But as we were putting the bikes away, I said to Oliver, "I thought she was quite nice really."

"Sure, well why shouldn't she have been?"

"I don't know. I thought she might seem more ... odd."

"Everybody's odd," he said.

"Yeah, only not so they're in mental hospitals." He shrugged.

"Did you like her stuff?"

"Quite a lot. I mean, I think she's good, didn't you?"

I nodded. "It's funny."

"What?"

"Don't you wish Mom did something ... like that? I mean, some real thing."

"She does real things!"

"No, you know what I mean. Some real profession where she was really involved in it and that sort of thing."

"That's not what Mom's like," Oliver said.

"I know that!" I said, exasperated, "But don't you ever *wish* she was some other way from the way she is?"

"She's fine the way she is," Oliver said.

I sighed. Maybe some day I'll have a son who thinks I'm fine just the way I am even if I weigh two hundred pounds or spend all day sitting in a corner twiddling my thumbs. Then I guess I'll look back on Oliver and understand. It's not, really, that I don't understand. Maybe it's just that since Mom and I are of the same sex, I worry more about my being like her when I grow up.

There's no reason I should be, I realize that. But I still worry about it. Also, I guess Oliver is just more content in general with The Way Things Are. Whereas I spend all my time brooding about The Way Things Could Be. Or Should Be. Probably his way is better.

More sensible, certainly.

Chapter Fifteen ⚡ The Day After

Tuesday, Ralph and Sara Lee went into New York so she could have her abortion. It's the kind where you come home the same day. That evening I ran into Ralph just as he was coming home.

"How'd it go?"

"Okay—no problems."

"Did it hurt?"

"A little."

I suddenly got very nervous. "How come? I thought it wasn't supposed to?"

"Well, they only give you a local anesthetic, you know."

"Ya, so?"

"So, nothing, Car. Listen, it didn't hurt much—don't get all excited."

"I'm not all excited. Where is she now?"

"She's at home, having dinner probably. Maybe you and Oliver could drop over to see her tomorrow. She did appreciate the thing of your ... wanting to pitch in. I think it did make her feel better."

"Ya, well, sure. Maybe we will then."

Since Wednesday wasn't a restaurant day, Oliver and I bicycled over around eleven-thirty in the morning. Sara Lee was in the kitchen with her mother, sitting at this round table they have and trimming radishes. Mrs. Takami has this really immaculate kitchen. I've never seen anything like it. I mean, if you even, like, leave an olive out, it would look very messy. That's how neat she is. She's a plump, quite pretty woman with black hair like everyone in the family, only hers is in a bun. Playing nearby were Yoko and Cordelia who are four and six. I sometimes babysit for them now that Sara Lee is away at college. They're both dolls. They have these perfectly round faces with big black eyes and shiny hair cut with perfectly straight bangs. They never look all messy and in blue jeans like most kids. Mrs. Takami always dresses them in these very pretty bright colored dresses. Today Yoko was in purple and Cordelia in orange. Yoko immediately crawled on my lap as I sat down. She's the cuddly, quiet one, Cordelia is more of an imp.

"Hi, Carla," Sara Lee said. "It's nice of you to come over."

She was peeling a radish, but in a very decorative way so it looked like a flower. I watched her hands which are long and white with perfect, moonshaped nails. It made me aware of my own ragged bitten ones.

"You have two more weeks to go with your restaurant?" Mrs. Takami asked. She always speaks in this very precise, quiet way. I just can't imagine her ever getting mad or doing anything wild.

"Yes. Gosh, I can't believe it's September already," I said.

I kept looking at Sara Lee. She looked so calm and composed. Of course, why shouldn't she be?

It's only in old-time movies that people lie around pale and fainting after abortions. Still, it was odd to think of. I'm sure she didn't tell her mother. Mrs. Takami would collapse if she knew about a thing like that. I wonder how Mom would take it if such a thing happened to me. Would I tell her or what?

Outside in the back, Ralph was playing ping pong with Henry. Henry is fantastically good at ping pong, like his father. He always beats Ralph although Ralph is pretty good too, by far the best in our family. Not that that says much, considering our general athletic ability. Oliver was sitting watching them. It was cool and quiet, just a touch of fall in the air. I kept thinking of the scene, including the one of Mrs. Takami, Sara Lee, and the little girls around the table, as a photo in a magazine: The Day After the Abortion. I know that even when things are calm on the surface, that doesn't mean there's no inner feeling. Sara Lee might have been feeling all sorts of things I don't know about. But it also seems like these events you expect to be so melodramatic never are. Whereas the little unexpected things that you don't notice at the time are what turn out to be important.

Maybe if Sara Lee and Ralph were to break up this year, the abortion would seem significant. But if, as is likely, they keep on going together, get married, and finally have a bunch of kids, I guess no one will even remember this or care about it. It's odd.

Chapter Sixteen ⚡ Ironing or Who Was Leonard Weisberg?

At the time, while we were at the Takamis', I felt fine. But somehow as the day wore on, I got into this really depressed mood. I realize I haven't exactly been on an even keel this summer, but this mood was a whopper. It made all the others look like small potatoes. I just felt mad at everyone and everything I could think of. I felt mad at Ralph for making Sara Lee pregnant, mad at Sara Lee for getting pregnant, mad at Oliver for never caring about things the way I do, mad at Dad for leaving, mad at Mom for not getting him back, mad at Marsha for being away all summer so I had no one to talk to. It's amazing, but I couldn't think of one single person I knew that I didn't feel like going over and socking in the stomach as hard as I could.

I thought of Bozo. Bozo was this big rubber clown Mom had gotten for me and Oliver when we were about six. She had said that whenever we felt mad at each other or at anyone we should go over and punch Bozo as hard as we wanted. At the time Bozo was about the size we were, maybe bigger. And it really had been a great feeling to just throw yourself at him and beat him up while he just bobbed back and forth with this dumb smile on his face. I wondered where he was. Probably in the attic or the cellar, if not given away. I wished I could find him; he was just what I needed.

By evening I was practically not speaking to anyone in the family. Oliver was off to see Letty and Ralph was at Sara Lee's, so no one even noticed what a lousy mood I was in. Which for some reason made me feel a lot worse. Finally at around ten I spotted the pile of laundry which Mom had left in the basket near the stairs. I don't get inspired to help out with the housework often, but ironing is something I enjoy. It's mindless like the blackberry picking, and being mindless seemed a good idea at the moment.

I dragged out the ironing board. I was just standing there, waiting for the iron to heat up, when Mom appeared.

"Oh Car, *you* don't have to do that," she said.

"Well, *someone* has to," I snapped.

Mom got this very hurt expression. "I was going to do it later," she said quietly.

I didn't say anything. I just picked up the iron and started ironing.

Mom was still standing there looking at me. "What's up, Car?" she said. "You seem to have kind of a chip on your shoulder lately."

I shrugged. "Nothing special."

This is going to sound ridiculous, but about two seconds later I heard myself saying, "It's just ... well, Sara Lee got pregnant and had an abortion, but she's OK, and—" I mean, here I'd gone around telling everyone especially *not* to tell their parents and here I went and did it. I don't know what possessed me. I guess I really wanted Mom's reaction. I mean, I do feel in a way that Oliver and Ralph look at it differently from me, not being of the same sex. Usually I would not say that, but in this case I think it was true.

"I'm glad she's okay," Mom said. "Poor thing, though." She sat down at the foot of the stairs. "You know, your generation is lucky, Car, really, they really are. Things are so much more open now. I remember when I had an abortion, the doctor was so nasty and cold. He made me feel so rotten, like I'd committed some heinous act. It was so humiliating! That was worse than the pain of it really."

I must have been standing there ironing the same corner of the tablecloth back and forth about a dozen times. My heart was beating like a drum. It was odd. Partly I felt like running full speed out of the room, I was so nervous. On the other hand, I was really glad Mom was telling me all this. Mom has always sort of favored Oliver. I've almost never, never felt she would tell me anything she wouldn't have told him. She must think I'm fairly mature to tell me this. That made me feel extremely good, despite the nervousness.

"You know, it's not easy to have an abortion, Car. I mean, even for me, believing in it, still I think there are always some mixed feelings ... Maybe if my mother had talked to me about those things, but she just never did. You and I don't always talk, but I feel like we can. I mean I hope if something like this ever happens to you, you'd

116

feel you could come to me.... I felt so lonely when it happened."

"Was that—a—did Dad want you to—" I stammered.

For a minute Mom didn't answer. I wondered if she had heard me. I wondered if she thought that was going too far, my asking that. Then suddenly in this quiet voice she said, "It wasn't Dad. It was a fellow named Leonard Weisberg. I hadn't even met Dad yet." She looked at me. "He was a student with me at City. You'd have liked him, Car. He was terribly brilliant, terribly—. Did I ever show you this picture of him?"

I shook my head.

In a flash Mom was up and raced out of the room to her room where she keeps these old pictures in an album. While she was gone, I remained in the same place. I felt like one of those George Segal sculptures: Girl Ironing.

In a minute Mom came back and shoved the picture at me. I looked at it. It was one of those cheap photos people take in subway stations for twenty-five cents. Leonard Weisberg had a long, thin face and was wearing glasses. He had big dark eyes. I don't think you could call him good-looking. I kept looking at his face, not knowing what to say. Finally I muttered, "Ya, he's very ... he has a nice face."

Mom took the picture back. "He died of Hodgkin's disease," she said. She was kind of fiddling with the picture, not looking at me. "It's funny, I gather now they have a cure for that or at least it's not so.... The amazing part was that

117

he knew he had it; they tried not to tell him, but he found out, he found some letter. But in spite of that he kept going to classes, just like anyone else, right up to the day they took him to the hospital the final time."

She sat down on the steps. "I remember I went to his house after he died. He had these books he wanted me to have. He lived with his sister. His parents died when he was young. Anyway, I just remember standing there in that dark hall with his sister watching me as I went through his books. She never liked me, really, and she had this awful, sour expression on her face. I felt like just running out or throwing the books at her. But I went through them anyway and took all I could carry. I still have them somewhere, I think."

The iron was on its side, fizzling quietly. I had stopped ironing; I was just watching Mom's face. I don't know if you've ever noticed this, but if you look at someone's face long enough, it's hard to judge any more if it's pretty or not. It just seems a face that could not be any other way, could not have any other hair or eyes. When Mom had been speaking, I had just kept imagining what she was saying. It was like a little movie running in my head. I saw Mom looking the way she does in these old photos we have—in saddle shoes and a longish skirt, her hair in a pony tail, standing in the dark hallway, and Leonard Weisberg's sister watching her, sort of a plump woman with her hair gnarled back in a bun, with little mean eyes.

There was this enormous pause. I stood there looking at Mom, and she sat there, her chin cupped in her hands, her eyes round and that funny freckled grey-brown color they are, looking straight ahead. I could see her swallow as though it was hard for her to talk. Maybe things like that seem very real, even twenty years later.

Suddenly she gave a kind of laugh. "Well, anyway, that's ancient history." But she didn't get up.

I had finally managed to finish one tablecloth. I pushed it over and reached for another one.

"It's funny," I said.

"Ya, well, life is funny, Car. It's not what you expect . . . whatever that is."

"I guess."

She smiled at me. "You'll do okay. Don't worry."

"I will?"

"Sure."

I hope that's true. Boy, do I hope that's true.

"Look, let me finish this ironing, will you? Go play the piano or something."

It was funny Mom mentioned that because I had just been thinking of the piano this afternoon. I used to take piano lessons, but since I've taken cello, I've let it slide. But at times I like to just sit down and boom out a few old pieces. The piano is out of tune, but it's a good one, an old Steinway. I opened it up and began playing Beethoven's *Pathetique*. It's a schmaltzy piece, but it's perfect if you're in a certain sort of mood.

I must admit I felt very good. Happy, even. Weak in the knees, true. I always thought that was just an expression, but when I walked away from Mom, my knees actually felt as though they were about to cave in. While I played, I thought of what she had said. I felt sorry about Leonard Weisberg. He did have a very nice face. As Mom had said, he looked like the kind of person I might have liked. But then I thought that if he had lived, Mom might have married him and then she would never have met Dad and I would never have been born. . . . It's selfish to look at it that way, but how else can you look at it, really?

As I said, I really do believe that Mom would not have told anyone else in the family these things. Maybe she never even told Dad—about Leonard Weisberg, anyway. What I liked was that she didn't say this is a secret, you must promise not to tell anyone. Somehow when people say that to me, it seems I always end up telling. Whereas here I felt it was just implied, that she felt she could trust me. And I really don't think I will tell anyone. Even Oliver. Even Marsha.

The other funny part, though, is to think of Mom having these love affairs or whatever before she met Dad. It certainly sounded like she was in love with Leonard Weisberg. I mean, I may not be objective but I think most people would agree Mom isn't exactly the sexy type. Even if you thought she was pretty or you liked her face, I don't think you'd say it was sexy. Of course, maybe that just doesn't matter all that much. I wonder if Leonard Weisberg was the only one. Of course, she did meet Dad when she was twenty.

Oliver came home at eleven just as I was pounding my way through Rachmaninoff's Prelude in B Flat. I like to use a lot of pedal and really throw myself into it. Especially if no one's around who can tell me about all the wrong notes I've hit.

"Ye Gods," was all Oliver said.

That sort of put a wet blanket on it. I stopped. "Hi, Ol—how's it going?"

He just looked at me, shook his head, and started upstairs.

Just wait. When I'm having a hot, rousing affair, I'll come in smiling enigmatically and won't tell him a darn thing.

That'll serve him right.

Chapter Seventeen ❧ Everything Is the Same and Everything Is Different

Dad is coming back. This is how I found out about it. I was walking down the stairs one day on my way to Marsha's. She just came back yesterday and we already had a marathon phone conversation, but barely touched on the essentials. So I was sort of racing out when Mom kind of popped out from the kitchen and said, "Car—Dad's coming back next week."

Next week! I wondered if she had known for awhile that he was coming back and had just waited to mention it or if he had just decided or what. "Oh, um, good," I said. "Um—permanently?"

She nodded.

I was sure she was going to add, "We'll see," or "Who can tell?" or "Let's play it by ear," but she said none of those things. But just as I was standing there, dumbfounded, not knowing what to say, she smiled mischievously and gave a little wink. Just a quick little wink. I'll probably spend the rest of my life figuring out what that wink meant.

I tore out of the house.

I decided not to mention about Mom and Dad to Marsha. The thing is, she left just before they separated and as long as they're getting back together now I don't know if I want to go into the whole thing. Some day I will, just not right now. Luckily, telling about the restaurant took long enough. Marsha was all admiration and said she and her parents would definitely come to the closing night which was to be this Sunday. The nice thing with Marsha is she always makes you feel that whatever you've done is one of the great achievements of the western world.

The next day Mom drove me over to the restaurant. Our purpose was twofold, as they say. I wanted to sit down in peace and quiet and work out exactly how we stood financially. Ralph had been good about saving all the slips when he'd ordered food, and Oliver and I had written down any time that we got anything extra. The problem now was to add it all up and then figure out everyone's salary. We'd decided at the beginning that salaries would be on the basis of how much we earned. I like this kind of thing, odd as that may seem, and for two hours I sat at one of the restaurant tables, multiplying, adding, crossing out.

While I did this, Mom was in the kitchen cleaning. Mom is funny about cleaning. Most of the time, ninety per cent of the time I'd say, she's an out-and-out slob. But occasionally she goes on these binges when she scours, scrubs, cleans closets, and is a madwoman. When I came in, finally going dizzy from looking at numbers for so long, she was flat on her belly, poking under the refrigerator with a broom handle.

"Mom, it wasn't that clean to begin with."

"No, but it was nice of the Stollingwells to lend you this place," she said. "I just want to—" But she straightened up and shook her head like a dog. "Yelp! I've had it, Car. Lemme out of here!"

We walked outside and before I knew it Mom was climbing my favorite tree, the one I'd been in when Oliver had gotten his brainstorm about the restaurant nearly three months ago. I climbed up after her. Once there, we just sat in silence, looking out over the hills. Finally, working up my courage, I said, "Why is Dad coming back?"

She smiled. "You mean, why did he go in the first place?"

"Well, both."

Mom wrinkled her nose. "I—I don't know how to explain it—I mean, it seems to me that, well, some people manage to find a job, a profession they really love, that satisfies them in every way. Or they don't but they don't care. Well, Dad does care only he never quite ... he's always wanted to do more."

"Like with his novel?"

"Right. And I guess it gradually was hitting him that he wouldn't and he felt kind of wretched."

That sounded so understandable to me that before I could stop myself I said, "But how come you're *not* like that?"

Mom laughed. "You mean, why don't I feel bad too—about my life?"

I nodded, awful though it sounded when she'd said it.

"I just don't," Mom said. "I don't know. Maybe I've just seen too many people who achieved things—including the kinds of things Dad thinks will make him happy—and they're not in such great shape. They just find some other thing to fuss about. I guess I, well, like I like things like sitting in this tree with you right now. That's the kind of thing I like."

"I'll never be like that," I said, really thinking aloud more than anything.

"No, I doubt you will, Car," Mom said. "And that's good in a way. You have much more drive than me—or than Dad either, really. So does Oliver in his own way. Like with actually doing this restaurant thing, not just sitting around dreaming about it."

I was silent a minute. "Do you think it'll be different now? For Dad, I mean?"

She shook her head. "I just don't know. I wish he could care less what people think, that's what I wish most. But he may just not be made that way."

"I'm glad he's coming back, though," I said.

Mom grinned. "So am I."

We climbed down from the tree. I walked just behind Mom to the car. The sun was shining on her hair, catching the grey as well as the blond. Maybe wanting to make up for asking those questions, but also really feeling it, I said, "I'm glad you didn't dye your hair, Mom—I like it this way."

"Thanks, hon."

Oliver says he always knew Dad would come back.

"But isn't it funny to think, Ol, that if Dad hadn't gone away we'd have gone to camp and never have had the restaurant at all?"

"So—be glad he went away."

"I can't be *glad* he went away. How could I?"

"Well, be glad he's back then."

"Of course I'm glad. I wish I hadn't read his novel, though."

Oliver just looked at me.

"I mean, I know it's silly to look up to your parents, but I used to think they were perfect—didn't you?"

"No," said Oliver calmly.

I sighed. "Mom says we have a lot of drive—that the restaurant was just a start, we'll go on to bigger and better things." I fattened up the compliment a bit.

"Sure. You'll be the first woman president and I'll—"

I made a face at him. "Well, I think it was a very nice thing to say."

But despite everything, I have this feeling everything has shifted just slightly, as though there'd been an earthquake overnight and you woke up to find all the furniture in different places. I just don't think I can think of Dad the same way after having read his novel or think of Mom the same way knowing about her love affairs and abortions and stuff, or about Ralph and Sara Lee the same way now that they had this crisis. I don't think I think the worse of any of them, but they all seem different to me.

The last night of *Chez Simon* was a lot of fun, however. The Stollingwells came and kept exclaiming over how great everything looked. The Pfeifers came and so did the Takamis and Mom and Dad and a lot of other people. For the first time we all ate, too. We put a whole bunch of tables together so we had one long table, and at the end we all helped Oliver cook the stuff and then served ourselves. It really tasted good. It's funny that we'd been serving it all summer without really tasting it. I had steak. I must admit I don't think I want to look at another trout for about eight hundred years.

The next morning I was up early. I don't know why—habit, I guess. I heard noise in the kitchen so I went down.

Mom and Dad were there standing near the refrigerator drinking glasses of grapefruit juice. They were in their grey sweatsuits and blue jeans. They are on this big physical-fitness kick and every morning they jog for an hour before breakfast.

"Hi!" I said.

"Hi, Car," said Dad. "How come you're up so early?"

I shrugged. I looked outside. It looked kind of grey and fallish. "It's supposed to rain," I said.

"We're protected," Dad said. At that, with one motion, they both pulled their hoods up over their heads and tied them under their chins. They looked like the Bobbsey twins. Then they set off. I could see them outside talking to each other. Mom is about a foot shorter than Dad and she was looking up at him sort of intently and he was listening. Then they started off, jogging slowly down the road. Pretty soon they disappeared from sight.

Oliver came into the kitchen in his pajamas and bathrobe. He began rustling around making breakfast. He's on this *café au lait* kick where he has to heat the milk separately and then pour it simultaneously with the coffee into a mug. It's quite a production and usually tastes quite good. "I think I'll start making bread this fall," he said. "I've never really gotten into bread."

"But Ol," I said suddenly. "Things will never be the same again! Never!"

"They were never that way to begin with," said Oliver, calmly measuring the milk.

"What way?"

"The way you imagined them to be."

Oliver the realist.

Someday, in about a thousand years, I, too, will be a realist.

Maybe.